BENEATH PERFECTION

A NOVEL BASED ON THE ORIGINAL SCREENPLAY **TREMORS** BY
S.S. WILSON AND BRENT MADDOCK
STORY BY S.S. WILSON, BRENT MADDOCK AND RON UNDERWOOD

CHRISTIAN FRANCIS

Contents

We were in the final stages of regaining the U.S. rights to our original screenplay for *Tremors*, released in 1990, when Christian Francis contacted us to point out that we also had the right to authorize a novelization—because Universal Studios had never done one. We immediately agreed to take advantage of his talents and track record and strike a deal.
The result you now hold, or view, or listen to.

There is much here to enjoy for even hardcore fans of the movie.

Working closely with us, and from an early longer draft of the script he found (that, ironically, we had not kept), Christian has converted the old classic to prose with many added details, new scenes, and new character moments.

Enjoy!
S. S. Wilson

T he desert stretched wide and silent under the unforgiving Nevada sun, so dry it made you thirsty just looking at it. Dust swirled lazily over cracked ground, while patches of brush huddled across empty gorges and valleys. In the distance, the mountains stood tall, soft and blue at the edges, but between here and there was nothing but cooked sand. It was an unrelenting place. Apart from the occasional vulture overhead, a scuttling scorpion, or a snake sliding, it was not a land for life to blossom. Unlike other verdant places where life teemed, here it didn't feel like life was waiting for anything. It felt like death had already passed through, and the land had simply given up. Then man came along and slapped a stretch of asphalt across it.

Down in the basin of one of the small valleys, a battered cabin stood off to one side of a dirt road, leaning against a big, ramshackle barn. Both structures stood as they had done for decades, and both seemed barely holding together like they might blow away if the wind ever dared pick up.

In front of the barn stood Edgar Deems. He was grizzled, stone-faced, and just as stubborn as the old mule he now walked around in circles outside of the barn. His whole life had been in this desert, and he had seen little beyond the town of Perfection that lay a mile to the east.

He ignored the world beyond. He had missed the coming and going of wars. He had no idea when the city banks failed, or when bread lines grew. He was raised in the remnants of the Great Depression, just as the Dust Bowl consumed middle America, and still, here in the valley, had no idea about a single thing. His life was spent working the meagre land he owned. The same his father owned before him. He drank whiskey like it was water and lived on a steady diet of beans eaten straight from a can and apples whittled down to the core with a short, dirty penknife.

With a large gray beard, stained yellow from decades of rolled cigarettes, he was often referred to as a hermit. Which suited him just fine. He was happy in his world, as it was a place without others, humans anyway. He wanted nothing to do with them. And when he *had* to speak to people, he did so like every word cost him money, and when he smiled, which wasn't often, it looked to others like it hurt.

And that is why the desert suited him. Nobody

bothered Edgar Deems, and Edgar Deems didn't much bother anybody else.

Justine, his mule, her head hung low, clopped lazily as he led her around by a rope.

Her ears were twitching, hearing a sound before he could.

He gave the rope a gentle tug as he looked worriedly at her. "C'mon, girl. Keep on movin'. You can do it."

But her ears twitched more, seeming agitated.

Edgar sighed… He knew what it meant.

The sound of a vehicle approaching could be heard long before it came into view.

As he turned, dreading who would be bothering him, Edgar breathed a sigh of relief. It was only Fred Green, towing a trailer full of sheep that bleated loudly.

Fred was someone as old and ornery as he was, and someone Edgar didn't mind passing the time with.

The truck ground to a stop in a cloud of dust, as Fred leaned out the window, his battered fedora stained around the brim with sweat. He noticed Justine and the look on Edgar's face. Without the need for pleasantries, he nodded to the mule.

"She doin' any better than yesterday?"

Edgar shrugged. "Still actin' up a bit. Seems like she wants to lay down, but won't find a place."

Fred nodded, then opened the driver's side door. Getting out, he reached back in and hoisted a bushel basket from the passenger seat. In it, fresh carrots spilled out.

"Well," he said, grinning, "I brung her something to make her feel better."

Edgar stared at the large bright vegetables. "Damnit, Fred, you can't give away all those. That's bucks waitin' to be had."

"Ah phooey, I got vegetables comin' out my ears. Usually, the varmints eat up half my crop. But lately I ain't so much as seen a gopher or a jackrabbit nowhere. Like they suddenly became allergic to what I'm growin'. But it's the sheep that I'm worried about."

Edgar looked at the trailer, to the sheep still bleating in a flurry. "They spooked too? You got a coyote problem again?"

Fred shook his head. "You'd think so, wouldn't ya? But there ain't any pack tracks that I can see. All just riled up over nothin', far as I can tell."

Fred placed the basket on the ground, and Edgar picked out a large carrot from it.

"Here ya go, girl," he said, handing it to Justine. "Look what Fred brought ya."

Half-hearted, the mule moved closer, and chewed on the bright orange end, as her tail swished weakly.

"We playin' cards tonight?" Fred asked.

"Nah, think I'll be sittin' up with her. Make sure she's okay."

Fred nodded. "Catch you Thursday, then? At mine? 7 o'clock?"

Edgar mimed tipping back a drink. "I'll bring the ammunition."

Tipping his hat, Fred smiled and climbed back into

his truck. Without another word, it rattled away, leaving Edgar and Justine alone again in the settling dust.

Edgar patted her flank. "Let's get you outta the sun for a spell, okay?"

But she didn't move. She just looked up at him.

He looked her in the eyes. "What is it? You been eating too much rabbit brush, again? Go on, you can admit it."

Without another word, he led her down to the rickety barn, her hooves dragging heavily. Inside, it was a fraction cooler out of the sun, yet still ripe with humidity and the musty smell of old hay and gasoline from a truck that had been parked inside.

Edgar shut the barn doors behind them and crossed to the long metal trough, still holding her rope.

"I'll get you some water, girl," he mumbled, as if she could understand him.

Alerted by something at her feet. Justine began to stamp on the wooden floorboards nervously. She looked down and let out a short, anxious bray.

Edgar turned, frowning. Justine's ears were totally flat now, and the lead rope between them was pulled taut.

"Hey, calm yer'self," he said.

The donkey brayed again, louder this time, hooves scraping against the floor.

Like a distant thunder, they both soon heard a low rumble. Somewhere beyond the barn walls. A strange noise amidst the otherwise calm day. A sound not on land, but underground.

Edgar did not have time to fill the trough, as the ground gave a sudden shudder, and the barn's wooden slat walls rattled.

"Damn 'quakes," he said, as dust sifted down from the rafters, dislodged by the vibrations. High in the eaves, a cluster of birds burst loose, wings thrashing as they escaped through a broken hole.

Justine huffed and stamped nervously.

"Hang on there, girl, I'll get us safe," he said as he rushed back toward the barn doors. He knew that he had to get outside, to get onto one of the large rocks, just like they always did when any earthquake decided to unceremoniously interrupt their lives.

He shoved the doors open, and as the bright sunlight fell inside, the rumble under the barn swelled into a roar. Under his boots, the floorboards shuddered more and more, as though a thousand snakes were slithering beneath. As they bucked under his boots, he grabbed hold of the door frame, letting go of Justine's rope. The floor cracked loudly, and sudden thin jagged lines came from under the barn and split the sandy ground outside.

In his sixty-eight years he had never seen an earthquake literally split the earth. Especially not in this valley that was normally sheltered by the surrounding bedrock.

As the ground split, a deafening noise sounded. A crash and a crunch all at once, then stopped as soon as it had come on. The barn had filled instantly with a thick cloud of dust. So much so that it blocked Edgar's vision and made him cough and wheeze. He could not see his truck, the trough, or Justine. Her whinnies and brays had stopped.

"Hey girl, you okay?" he spluttered.

It was the smell that hit him next. A sudden thick and foul odor, which caused him to gag, and almost lose his breakfast. He yanked a handkerchief from his pocket and immediately covered his nose and mouth.

"Justine," he called out again, as he stepped into the barn.

He quickly stopped again as his boot scuffed across something wet beneath him.

"Huh?"

Inside, the haze had begun to settle.

Through the dust, just a few yards in front of him, he saw that the floorboards had cracked outwards, leaving a ten-foot hole, and the ground beneath it. Ground that had been churned.

"What in the name of Jehovah," he whispered.

The sunlight from outside soon illuminated the details within the dissipating cloud of dust. Beyond the floorboard and dirt was something else—blood spatters. Heavy streaks that coated the floor, the walls, and even the side of his parked truck. Redness, thick with chunks of meat and matted hair.

"Jesus, no," Edgar croaked weakly, blinking repeatedly, trying to clear this scene from his vision. He gasped, refusing to believe what he was seeing.

Instinctively, he turned and reached to where a loaded Winchester rifle hung above the door frame.

Without a pause, he cocked the weapon, checking it was loaded. Of course it was.

No more tremors were felt through his boots.

Turning around he looked outside, across the bright sand and rock, and inside over the blood and wrecked floor.

But he saw nothing.

Nothing that could have done this.

Chapter 1

Rock, Paper, Scissors

The sun lit the rough stone, dry scrub, and the steep cliff that dropped a thousand feet to the valley floor.

Up on a high plateau, silhouetted against the baking heat, Valentine McKee stood barefoot and shirtless. He wasn't contemplating the sunrise. His mind was busy with more pressing morning questions, like whether some unlucky bug or lizard far below was currently getting hosed by the arc of his morning piss. A critter now having the worst day of its little life.

Val was twenty-five, and was smart enough and good-looking enough to have made something of himself. Instead, he'd coasted through his life like a tumbleweed, going wherever the wind blew him. And that wind had dumped him here, in a dusty, nowhere corner of Nevada. He was an underachiever at an almost Olympian level, ruthlessly following the path of least resistance for every single moment he encountered. But now, as he zipped up his fly, he began to wonder again why he hadn't taken more risks in life.

Away from the edge, a few sleepy cows blinked at him from a patch of grass, chewing cud and swatting flies with their tails. Val scratched his bare chest as he yawned, wandering back to the pickup truck parked nearby. An old relic of the swingin' sixties, the truck was a heap of rust that somehow still managed to work. The door bore the faded, hand-painted letters: *V & E — All Type's of Job's.* The misplaced apostrophes had never bothered anyone enough to fix, mainly as no one in Perfection had any idea that they were wrong.

The truck bed was crammed with tools, spare parts, and countless rolls of duct tape. These were also all kinds of odds and ends used for quick fix-up jobs. And lying among these, wrapped in an old, stained sleeping bag, was Earl.

Earl Bassett, whose harsh snoring now sounded like a broken chainsaw.

Val rapped his knuckles lightly against the side panel of the truck.

"Good morning, Mr. Bassett," he said in a whisper. "This is your mornin' wake-up call. Time to move that fat ass of yours, so we can make some money."

No response, except another long, loud, guttural snore.

With a humph, Val looked around. He slowly eyed the cows, as they stared back, chewing lazily in the sun, and he couldn't help but grin.

Mischievously, he climbed onto the truck's bumper,

careful not to let a single creak of rusty metal give him away.

He bounced lightly, just enough to make the suspension sway.

With a burst of energy, he threw all his weight down then up, down then up, violently rocking the truck from side to side. He had to fight his desire to laugh as he hollered: "Stampede! Earl! Stampede! The cows! They're comin' right for us! Get outta the way!"

There was a mumbled curse and a furious thrashing from the sleeping bag as Earl, still very much half-asleep, rolled straight out of the truck bed, and landed hard in the dirt. He clambered to his feet, breathless in a panic.

He saw the cows. They hadn't budged an inch since nightfall.

Val couldn't hold his laughter anymore.

"You dumb shit," Earl grumbled, rubbing his eyes.

At forty-three, Earl was a good old boy through and through. Like Val, he had also drifted from job to job his whole life and had the wrinkles and rough hands to prove it. Unlike Val though, Earl knew exactly why he hadn't made much of himself. Bad luck. That was what he chalked up all his misfortune to. And he never missed a chance to pass yet another story about it along, whether Val wanted to hear it or not.

"You know," Earl said, brushing dust off his jeans. "I was in a stampede once."

Val chimed in without missing a beat. The two of them reciting it word for word:

"Three hundred heads going hellbent for the horizon..."

Earl caught himself too late… he'd been baited.

"How many cows you reckon it takes to make a stampede, Earl? Is it like, three or more? And more to the point… is there a minimum speed they gotta be at before it gets downgraded from a stampede to brisk walk?"

"I wish a stampede on your ass," Earl growled. He patted his pockets for cigarettes but came up empty, except for an old Zippo lighter.

Val was busily looking for a cigarette of his own and had managed to find a crumpled pack from his back pocket, but he found no lighter.

Without speaking as they saw each other's predicament, then traded: a cigarette for the lighter.

On the open tailgate, a battered Coleman stove sat with a coffee pot on it.

Earl reached for it, put his hand on the side, and immediately grimaced.

"Cold?" he said, turning back to Val. "And what? No breakfast either?"

"Hey, I did it yesterday," Val replied. "Franks and beans, remember?"

"The hell you did. It was…" Earl thought deeply for a moment. "Eggs! I did eggs. Right?"

"When I'm your age, I'll probably forget what I ate, too," Val said, shaking his head.

With his buttons successfully pushed, Earl immediately raised his fist to Val. A threatening move.

Val mirrored him immediately, and they launched into how they resolved all their conflict. With a simple game of rock-paper-scissors. No arguing, no best two out of three. No moods. No screaming. One shot won. And both lived by the result. That was the rule of their life.

Without a word they both played.

Val threw paper. Earl threw scissors.

Scissors cut paper.

Scissors won.

Earl won.

With a moan, Val trudged over to the Coleman stove to start pumping up its fuel tank, resigned to being the one who would make coffee and breakfast.

As midday came around, and many cups of coffee later, Val and Earl were slap bang in the sun's glare, on a job.

They were standing at the edge of a road, along an endless line of barbed wire fencing. Fencing they had been tasked to fix a section of.

A few horses watched them from a distance, and to Val it seemed as if they were judging the quality of their fence fixing.

Earl pulled the wire taut, then yelped as a barb punched through his glove.

"God damn!" he said through gritted teeth. "Is this really a job for intelligent men?"

Val laughed. "Show me one and I'll ask him."

Taking off his glove, Earl sucked at the puncture on

his palm. "Damnit," he grumbled. "I keep thinking," he said. "If we were even half-serious about making money, we'd quit being hired hands and—"

"Handymen, Earl," Val said. "We're *handymen*. Get it straight."

"Yeah, yeah, whatever," Earl shook his head. "We oughta quit being handymen and get ourselves some *real* employment. Some jobs that pays the bucks. Not stand out here getting roasted as we fixed a damn fence."

Val leaned on a fence post, wiping sweat from his forehead. He then swept his arm out toward the endless, empty desert around.

"What, and give up all this personal freedom?" He said, only half-serious. "I don't know, man. Seems like a hell of a price to pay. Get a real job, get trapped in a glass office working for an asshole. At least here, you're the only asshole I gotta deal with."

Earl nodded with a laugh. "Right back atcha."

"But yeah, I get it," Val added. "We gotta do something, right? It's time?"

Earl shrugged as he put his glove on and went back to fixing the fence.

The '60s Jeep Gladiator bounced its way down the narrow jeep trail. The pickup was like a battered ship caught in a rocky sea. Val wrestled the steering wheel, riding the brakes, shifting through gears, and leaning halfway out the window as he navigated his way around the dips and divots in the rough path ahead.

Earl had wedged his boots against the dashboard and was calmly munching a raw hot dog straight from its out-of-date package, entirely unconcerned about the bone-jarring ride. Quite content to let Val do the work. With his sweat-stained trucker's hat pulled down low, Earl could quite easily fall asleep right now.

"This goddamn trail gets worse every day," Val moaned.

Earl nodded, his mouth full of warm meat. "Had a lot of rain I guess."

He then reached under the seat and pulled out a battered box of Hershey bars. Something that immediately caught Val's attention.

"Oh, damn yeah," Val said, keeping one eye on the uneven trail.

Inside the box, though, there was only one bar left.

Earl sighed, knowing what was coming.

As soon as Val saw the bar, he raised his fist without a word.

The Challenge. Again.

Earl had no choice. You always had to accept the challenge.

One, two, three.

Val threw rock. Earl threw scissors.

Rock beat scissors.

Val won.

Earl groaned as he plucked the lone candy bar and

turned to the now grinning Val. Without a thought, he unwrapped the bar, then jammed it into Val's mouth.

Val didn't care. He won.

As the truck hit a small ditch, it lurched, and the empty box on Earl's lap fell into the footwell.

"Watch it," he said, pointing ahead. "You're gonna get us hung up on a damn rock."

"Hey, don't talk to the driver when he's concentrating," Val barked back, chewing the candy bar in his open mouth.

But the warning came too late, and Val was not paying enough attention, as the truck pitched a sharp drop. Its chassis slammed down hard onto the dirt with a loud *thwonk*, jolting both of them out of their seats. The pickup quickly shuddered, and the engine cut out.

Val shot Earl a dirty look, still chewing on the candy. "See what you did?" he grimaced.

Earl just shook his head and opened the door. "Get the shovel," he grumbled.

Both climbed out, grabbed a shovel from the truck bed, and moved their high-lift jack, to start the familiar process of getting the truck unstuck.

It wasn't long until they were bouncing once more down the trail and soon out onto a more level road. As the truck left the dirt and hit the level concrete, the wheels hummed gratefully.

Val relaxed a little as he let the truck pick up speed. "So, what else we gonna be doin' today?"

Earl removed his trucker's hat and pulled out a

crumpled scrap of paper from inside. He read his handwritten scrawls from it.

"Damn," he said, "It's garbage day."

"Aw man, already?" Val groaned. "What's Nestor paying us for that then?"

"Fifty bucks… and that's forty-seven more than we got."

Drumming his fingers on the wheel, Val thought for a second. "Hey, Burt and Heather's place is closer, right? Why don't we do their linoleum today. Garbage can wait 'til tomorrow."

"Nestor's out of town tomorrow," Earl replied. "So, if we don't dig today, we don't get paid today…"

Val didn't look convinced. Mainly as he hated working at the dump—or as Nestor called it a 'waste disposal site'. That name to Val was too flashy for a hole in the ground they threw trash into.

Earl shook his head. "Dammit, Valentine, you never plan ahead. You *never* take the long view. Hell, it's only Monday and I'm already working on Wednesday." He then squinted at the scrap of paper once more, this time unsure of what he wrote. "Wait. It *is* Monday, right?"

Val wasn't listening. He was staring out at the desert, squinting against the sun. Seeing something ahead.

A hundred yards down the road, a little Toyota pickup sat to one side. Beside it, a lone figure waved an arm high, trying to flag them down.

"Who the hell is that?" Val asked. "Is that… what's-his-name? That grad student?"

"Nah, he graduated. Must be the new one."

"The new one? Already?" Val's eyebrows raised. I heard it's supposed to be a girl, right?"

Earl didn't even have time to brace himself before Val jerked the wheel. The truck shot off to the dusty shoulder of the road, rattling across the scrub at full throttle.

As they bumped wildly over the ground, Val muttered under his breath, almost like a prayer: "You *will* have long blonde hair, big green eyes, nice full breasts that stand up and say *hello...* And you'll have an ass that won't quit, and legs... legs that go all the way up."

"Where else would legs go? Ya damn savage," Earl said as he held on, watching the desert fly past in a cloud of dust as the truck skidded to a halt behind the Toyota.

The cloud soon rolled away, and Val leaned forward eagerly, trying to see the dream girl from his mind walk up.

His hopes sank.

There was Rhonda LeBeck. She looked about Val's age, twenty-five or so, but that was about where the resemblance to his daydream ended. Her hair was pulled back messily under a baseball cap, and thick glasses sat on her nose. A smear of white zinc oxide streaked across her face like war paint, protecting her skin from the harsh rays of the sun. She looked like the type who brought her own bottled water to a bar. She was not the kind of woman Val had any interest in. He preferred them as dumb as he thought he was.

As they got out of the truck, Val put on his Stetson.

Rhonda marched right, sticking out her hand enthusiastically. In her other hand she held a broken piece of equipment with wires hanging out from all sides.

"Hi, I'm Rhonda. Rhonda LeBeck," she said brightly, giving Val's hand a firm shake. "I'm up here for the semester. I—"

"Yeah, yeah, all that geography," Earl interrupted, walking around the front of the truck.

"Geology," Val corrected.

"Um, actually it's seismology," Rhonda clarified, smiling. "Earthquakes to be more specific. And you both... Well, you have to be Val and Earl, right? I've heard so much about you."

"Earl and Val," Earl said dryly with a straight face. "And we deny everything. Unless it's how damn good lookin' we are."

Rhonda laughed, pushing her glasses up higher on her nose.

"Listen, I got a question for you two," she said. "Do you know if anybody's doing any blasting or drilling or anything like that around here? Like up to fifty miles away?"

Val laughed. "Around here? Why would anyone do that? There's nothin' here to blast, unless you really hate sand and rock."

"Well, I'm supposed to monitor these seismographs that have been installed along the basins," Rhonda explained, holding up the broken equipment in her other hand. "You know, they measure vibrations and everything..."

"Yeah," Val said, nodding. "Vibrations in the ground."

"Right. But I've been getting some *really* strange readings. I mean, the school's had these machines up here three years and they've never recorded anything like this. Maybe a small tweak of a needle now and then... But now... the readings are just weird. So, it's either someone is drilling or something, or they're on the fritz." She motioned to the one in her hand. "I took this one apart, and it all seems fine. Did some tests. All good... Hence me asking about the blasting. They are reading *something* big."

"Is there an earthquake coming?" Earl asked, feeling a bit worried by the prospect.

Rhonda shook her head. "No, the readings are too short, and not as deep. They read like fifty feet down max."

Earl scratched the back of his neck. "Well, we'll ask around. Let you know if we hear anything. But we ain't heard squat about squat."

Val motioned behind him. "There's that highway work about five miles thataway, but don't think they're doing much."

Earl nodded.

"Well thanks anyway," Rhonda said with a grateful smile. "God, I hope the machines aren't screwed up. I might have to bag the whole semester, 'cause they won't replace these anytime soon... Anyway, sorry to flag you down to ask you that, but there's not a lot of people around here."

"No problem at all," Earl said with a smile. "Nice meeting you, ma'am Hope you get it all sorted out."

Val tipped his Stetson with a casual flick, (acting a cowboy when he sure as hell wasn't one), and then climbed back into the truck.

With an amused smile, Rhonda watched them drive away. That smile soon fell as she turned back to her own truck and caught sight of her reflection in the window. She winced, seeing the bright white streak across her nose.

"Oh, strong look, Rhonda," she said. "They must have thought you're a damn idiot."

"Ma'am?" Val laughed. "You called her ma'am?"

"What? It's polite," Earl said. "It's gentlemanly!"

Val laughed harder.

Earl did not. "You know, if you wanted to, if *you* were a gentleman too, we could take a look at those seismograms for her."

"*Graphs*, seismo*graphs!*" Val corrected, still laughing, as he gave him a sideways glance. "Besides, what the hell do *we* know about seismographs?"

"Bupkis, but that ain't the point," Earl said with a sudden chuckle. "It sure might be a slick way of you getting to know her."

"Get to know her? Why do I want that?"

Earl let out a groan of frustration. "Goddammit,

Valentine, you won't go for any gal unless she fits that damn list of yours, top to bottom, will ya?"

"Well, sure," Val replied. "What's the use in having a list if you don't follow it? Not much of a list is it? Besides I'm sure she has one. College educated. Hedge fund manager. Holidays in the Hamptons."

"That is dumber than my ass," Earl added. "Just because she's intelligent? A total opposite to someone like that Bobby Lynn Dexter you were seein'."

"Bobby?" Val said, looking offended. He flipped down the truck's sun visor, and there taped to it were a half-dozen snapshots of nearly identical young women. Long blondes with vacant stares, toothy smiles, and big voluptuous breasts breaking out of tight tops. He jabbed a finger at one.

"*Tammy* Lynn Baxter," he said, as if that explained everything.

"Don't matter what her name is," Earl said. "They're all the damn same. Dead weight with dead heads. 'Ooh! I broke a nail!'… They all made my skin crawl. At least that woman back there was real!"

Val shrugged. "Well, I'm a victim of circumstance, what can I say? And that circumstance comes with a D cup and daddy issues."

"Victim of your pecker more like," Earl moaned.

He sank deeper in his seat, shaking his head. "Look, don't make the same mistake I made Val. Twenty years I was looking for a woman exactly like Miss October 1968. And where'd it get me? Here. With you. In a truck. Not having had a shower for a week."

Val rolled his eyes. "Sweet baby Jesus, give me mercy."

The truck rattled along the cracked blacktop, heading to the scattered buildings that made up the town of Perfection, Nevada.

It was a town that some people could call a small hamlet, yet that others may call the ass end of nowhere. Just a handful of houses and trailers huddled together for shade beneath a wide, pitiless sky. Its only landmark was an aging, wood-framed water tower that stood in the middle of the town.

As they turned onto the main dirt strip that ran through the town, they passed a weather-beaten sign: *PERFECTION — Pop. 14.* An outdated sign that not only included those like Edgar Deems who lived a couple of miles out of town, but also a few that had been dead for a few years. No one was in a hurry to correct it though.

The heart and soul of the town was Walter Chang's general store. The sign out front, in both English and Chinese, advertised: *Groceries, Haircuts, Post Office, Town Hall, VIDEOS!* Catering to so few people meant that it sold whatever was needed. And being the only shop in a town where there was no bank, it didn't always sell for money. Walter's was open to a trade, not that he would ever be fair in any exchange.

The store had been standing for over a century, its worn wooden shelves and warped glass counters holding generations of stories. A faded sepia photograph hung behind the register, two stern-faced figures in old-world dress: Pyong Lien Chang and Lu Wan Chang. They were the original founders, opening the store in the late 1800s to serve miners, cattlemen, and anyone desperate or foolish enough to settle in the valley. And it had stayed in the Chang family ever since. Walter, born in China and raised there until his teens, was their great-nephew. After his parents stayed behind, he immigrated to the U.S. and eventually took over the store from more distant relatives who'd grown tired of Perfection's heat and emptiness. But Walter, he fit in just fine. This was a world he loved, and one he could make a few bucks in.

Val and Earl pulled the truck outside of the store, next to a camouflage-painted, 4x4 Chevrolet Blazer. As they got out, their attention was caught by Melvin Plug, the town's teenage pain-in-the-ass, who was casually bouncing his basketball off the parked cars as he walked toward them. As he got closer, with the basketball hitting car after car, Earl pointed a warning finger at him.

"Melvin, you touch our truck and you die, you got me?"

Melvin snorted, giving them a theatrical shiver. "Oh, man, I'm really quaking in my boots! An old man will break a hip coming after me!"

Earl sneered. "You'll be quaking when I shove those boots knee deep in your ass!"

Melvin gave their truck a wide berth.

"Earl?" Val asked quietly, joking. "He'll quake with *his* boots, up to *his* knees, in *his* own ass? How the hell does that work?"

"Huh?"

"Or is it *your* knees in his ass, and *you'll* be wearin' his boots?"

"I'll shove his boots in your ass too if you're not careful," Earl said, as he turned and walked into the store.

"Buy me dinner first," Val called out after him.

Inside the store, Walter Chang bustled behind the counter, keeping a watchful eye on everything. A small flickering television affixed to the wall behind him droned on, showing what was either a nature documentary about the food chain or some local pest control ad; it was hard to tell.

At the small bar sat Burt and Heather Gummer, looking exactly like what they were: survivalists waiting for the end of the world. Burt, square-jawed and meticulously spoken even in casual conversation, shoved a box of bullets across the counter to Walter.

"Sure, Walter, these *are* hollow points, but they're not the Hydra-Shok hollow points I asked for," he said sternly. "That's what I ordered, and that's what I want and I won't settle for anything less."

Walter blinked, staring at the box. "I'm sorry Burt, I thought bullets were bullets. If it bangs and buries, it's good enough." He spoke with a thick Chinese accent, despite having been in the country for most of his life. Shaking his head, he picked up the box and placed it on a shelf behind. He knew better than to argue with Burt Gummer. Not that Burt would cause harm, but he was an immovable man, and would not be beaten into buying something he didn't want. Unlike Val and Earl, who were easy to manipulate.

At that exact moment, as if he conjured them here by thinking of them, Val and Earl stepped through the door. Immediately Walter smiled as he reached into the fridge, pulled out two bottles of beer and popped the caps off them. By the time they came in and reached the counter, the bottles were ready and waiting.

"Hi, guys," Heather said, smiling warmly, resting her arm on the assault rifle that lay on the bar in front of her. "What you been up to?"

"Ran into that new college student," Val said, accepting his beer. "That Rona girl."

"Rhonda," Earl corrected. "She's getting some kind of strange readings on her thingys."

"Strange readings?" Burt grunted, suddenly looking annoyed. "You know, if those kids turn up oil or uranium or something out there, next thing the Feds'll be at *our* door, kickin' them in with their size 12 jackboots, telling us all 'Sorry, time to move outta town. Eminent domain. You don't get a penny.'"

"Down, honey, down," Heather said soothingly.

Val grinned and took a swig from his beer. "Yeah, Burt. The way you worry, you're gonna have a heart attack before you get the chance to survive World War Three."

Walter and Heather laughed, but Burt only gave a thin smile.

Earl wasn't paying attention. He was too busy enjoying his beer.

Suddenly the compressor on the ice cream freezer kicked on the far side of the room. It sounded with a loud chugging. One that ended in a high-pitched squeal that even rattled the glass jars on the shelves.

Walter motioned at it hopefully. "Hey, guys, listen. Whaddya think? Bearing going out?"

"Could be." Val grabbed his beer and stepped nearer to the freezer to investigate, but just then Earl threw an arm out to block him.

"We'll swing by later, and have a look then, okay Walter?" Earl said. "We got a schedule we gotta keep."

"Right," Val agreed with mock seriousness. "We plan ahead, didn't you know that, Walter? That's why we came in here. 'Cause we are so busy. Earl explained it all to me."

"We just came in here for a pack of smoke," Earl added, taking out a five dollar note and putting it on the counter. "We can come back later and have a look."

Walter sighed a silent 'Fine'. He reached under the counter and slid a pack of cigarettes over to him. "I'll get your change when you come back." he said.

Earl smirked. "Fair deal," he said.

As they turned to leave, something on one of the shelves caught Val's eye. He stopped short, staring at it blankly. It was a bleached cattle skull, mounted neatly on a wood base, a crisp tag hanging from one horn asked for *$29.95*.

"Hey, what the hell is this, Walter?" Val asked incredulously.

Burt beamed proudly. "A beauty, isn't it? We bought three of 'em for the rec room."

Val walked back over to the counter and lowered his voice to a whisper. "We sold 'em to you for three frickin' bucks a piece, and you're selling 'em for thirty?"

"And I appreciate it," Walter replied with a smile.

"But we were supposed to be ripping *you* off as we just found 'em out there." Val said. "But thirty damn bucks!?"

Before Walter could reply, a car alarm blared from outside.

Burt was through the door in a flash.

Val and Earl followed, grinning as Heather picked up the rifle from the counter and followed, shaking her head.

Out front, Melvin was backing away from Burt's Blazer, hands raised in surrender with a worried expression. The basketball rolled on the ground nearby.

Burt stormed over. "Melvin, you little asshole!" he shouted. "Not the blazer. Never the blazer! There's ordnance in there that could have blown you sky high!"

"It wasn't me, man!" Melvin yelped. "Your truck's just screwed up, that's all!"

Burt pressed the button on his alarm fob and the

blaring suddenly stopped. He shot Melvin a second glare that promised future consequences.

Val and Earl walked back into their truck, chuckling at the situation.

"Why don't his folk ever take him to Vegas with 'em?" Val asked as he started the engine.

"You gotta ask *that*?" Earl laughed. "Would you wanna take that pissant on holiday with you?"

"Point taken."

Not even a hint of a breeze stirred the desert.

On a lonely slope of packed earth, far from the town, the ground gave a tiny shiver.

Without any audible noise, loose dirt and small pebbles began to trickle down the embankment, sliding in aimless streams, as something or some*things* moved beneath the surface.

Miles away, a rusted old car sat forgotten in the sand, its paint long since seared off by the scorching heat. It seemed as lifeless as the rocks that lay around it, until the hood gave a faint shudder and began to clack as it shook.

As the vibrations coursed through across the desert, life above continued, oblivious to any of it.

Just outside of Perfection lay the dump, a place where all the trash for a hundred miles came to die, or more factually, get buried in one of the huge pits.

Earl fought with the levers of a bulldozer that was older than he was, as its massive scoop pushed along mounds of buzzing, fly-choked garbage into a nearby pit. The machine groaned with every pass, and the stench from the mass of rotten, sun-baked garbage was very tough to breathe.

Val moaned as he walked nearby, hurling bulging black bags and broken odds and ends into the pit as fast as he could.

Despite both sweaty men wearing kerchiefs tied across their mouths and noses, it did nothing to stop the stink from making their stomachs turn. But they focused on one thing: money was money, and money is what they needed.

It certainly was dirty, miserable work, but when the last mound of trash was cast into the hole, Earl shut down the bulldozer's engine with a relieved sigh. The machine also gave a final wheeze as if it agreed with him that enough was enough.

Across the other side of the hole, the shade of an abandoned truck trailer offered a rare oasis. A steel beast that had once hauled heavy rock loads, now it sat mired in cracked dust and weeds, with tires that were flattened long ago. Underneath this large frame, an old sofa waited like a reward for their efforts.

And just as they did after every job they worked here, Earl and Val flopped down gratefully onto the sofa, passing a gallon jug of warm water between them.

The sound of a car approaching caught their attention, but neither could be bothered to turn to see who it was. They were too hot, bothered and exhausted.

It was Nestor Cunningham driving his old Cadillac. With one arm resting casually out the window, he surveyed their work. He gave a slow nod of approval as he caught their tired gazes.

"Looking good, fellas," he said. "You do one hell of a professional job. Now lemme have that bill when you got a second."

Val and Earl exchanged a weary glance, then started patting themselves down for pen and paper. Earl came up with a handful of crumpled receipts but no pen. Val produced three different pens but no paper. Typical.

After a moment of frustrated fumbling, they swapped supplies without a word, and Earl scribbled out a rough invoice on the back of one of Walter's receipts.

He then stood up and took it over to the Cadillac.

"It's fifty bucks between you, right?" Nestor asked, as he tucked the scrawled paper into his shirt pocket. "Twenty-five apiece? Now, I'll have to give it to you on the first of the month. Okay?"

The two men exchanged looks of annoyed disbelief.

Earl opened his mouth to protest, but Nestor cut in.

"Now, you know I'm good for it," he said quickly. "And I always have work for you, that I could give to others."

"Yeah, we know," Val replied, containing his anger.

"But if you're really short, you're welcome to dinner anytime at my trailer. I'd enjoy the company."

Before they could answer, he shifted the Cadillac into gear and trundled off, leaving nothing but a cloud of dust for them to stand in.

Val stood up as he watched Nestor go. He then shook his head and kicked the side of the sofa.

"What the hell happened?" Val moaned. "Are we too Goddamn easy-going?"

"No, Nestor hasn't got a choice," Earl replied. "This whole town is… what do they call it? Economically depressed? At least we *will* get paid."

"What I don't get. If Nestor has this place, that always has stuff to do. Then he *has* money, right?"

"We don't know that."

"He lives in a damn trailer in town. Why not a house? What happens to all his money? I'll tell you what, he keeps it. He *has* fifty bucks. He's just a dick."

Earl smirked. "As my momma used to say, the richest of the paupers is still a pauper."

"What the hell is that supposed to mean?"

"Damned if I know," Earl suddenly laughed to himself.

As they ambled back to their truck. Earl fished in his pockets for the keys.

Val was doing the same, but was looking for a lighter for the cigarette dangling from his lips. As usual, Val found the keys but no lighter. Earl found the lighter but no keys.

They traded without a word.

"Okay… So, what if we just did it?" Val said, lighting up. "Today. Move down to Bixby. Get serious."

"We could," Earl replied. "Sure, we could. But we'd have to get real serious. It costs twice as much to rent a place down there. And Nestor ain't payin' us now for a week."

Val took a long drag as he thought. "So? We could just screw it all today, count the fifty as a loss, and just go. That car wash pays good. They're always looking for people."

Earl gave him a sidelong glance as he opened the truck door. "Car wash? If we're gonna take the plunge, we oughta have a better plan than that. And fifty is a lot to leave hanging. We gotta plan this right."

"Yeah, sure, plan," Val said. "You go ahead and plan it... for another year or two."

As they drove to town, the road ahead of them still looked the same as always, wide, dusty, and leading to nowhere.

CHAPTER 2

BAD VIBRATIONS

Earl crouched on a folding ladder, tools clinking on the metal roof, squinting at the fan housing of an air conditioner on top of a trailer.

"God almighty," he muttered. "Thing's older than I am."

Val, at the base of the ladder, laughed. "What isn't?" he quipped. With one foot on the bottom rung, he was happy doing this job. All he had to do was make sure Earl didn't fall.

The AC unit gave a sudden cough and groaned to a stop.

Earl shook his head and came down from the ladder. "Well, we can't fix it now. Need a new fan," he said.

Then, a new noise kicked up, a high-pitched staccato barking, fierce and furious, like machine-gun fire from a tiny gun.

Val turned just in time to see it: Viola's dog, a

minuscule, bug-eyed gargoyle of a creature that looked like it had been wound too tight at the factory. It came tearing around the corner, leash dragging behind loosely.

It launched itself at Earl's boots, teeth flashing.

"Aw, hell no!" Earl gasped, staggering backward.

Val could not contain his laughter.

The little dog, barely bigger than a boot, danced in circles, snapping at Earl's heels as he backed away like this tiny dog was a bear.

"You see that?" Earl cried. "It's got murder in its eyes!"

Val was doubled over now. "You're scared of a dog you could punt into next week!"

"I'm scared of anything that angry and under two pounds," Earl shot back, pointing. "That's not natural."

From the porch, Viola appeared, prim in a pressed floral blouse and slacks, holding a tall glass of iced tea like she hadn't noticed the chaos at all.

"Bad girl!" she scolded gently, tugging the leash up. The dog wriggled in her arms, still snarling like it had unfinished business. "She gets a little worked up around strangers," she added, smiling sweetly. "I keep telling my son to take her back, but he's always too busy. And I'm stuck here with her!"

"Thing's a menace," Earl said.

Viola ignored the comment and motioned to the top of the trailer. "What's the diagnosis, doc?" she asked.

"Fan's shot. Gonna need a whole new unit."

Viola sighed. "Well, if it's not one thing, it's the other."

"We'll order one from Walter, sure he can find a used one for cheap."

As they walked back to the truck, the little dog still barked at them from the trailer's doorway.

"Man, I tell you what," Val muttered. "Whatever's next on the list, it better be an improvement."

Earl smiled. "It's a real shit job next."

"It can't be that bad can it?"

"No… A real shit job. We got a cesspool to empty."

Val sighed. "Aw…. Shit."

The pump was ancient, dented, and smelled every bit as bad as the sludge it was designed to haul. A faded stencil on the metal side read: *Chang's Pump-U-Rent.* It was a decrepit machine that gurgled continuously and ominously, leaking brown water from its cracked fittings.

On their third job of the day, behind the Plug's family trailer, Val and Earl knelt by the intake valve. They wrestled with the heavy, slimy hose like it might attack them if they loosened their grips. Both had expressions that reflected their deep regret about taking this job, as they jammed the nozzle into the open top of the trailer's cesspool, ready to suck out the filth inside.

Through the screen door of the trailer, loud, awful heavy metal music blared across the dirt lot. Melvin Plug lounged on a lawn chair outside, tossing a basketball lazily between his hands, grinning at the worker's misery.

"Hey, Melvin," Val called over, still struggling with the hose, "you *could* lend a hand, you know? Most of this shit's yours, anyway."

Melvin didn't even pretend to care as he ignored the comment. "Listen, if you guys buy me a six-pack, I'll pay ya for it. Give you an extra two bucks as well!"

Earl glanced back and gave him a long, serious look. "Son, beer is for adults."

Melvin sulked quietly as he looked away. He bounced his basketball hard against the side of the trailer.

Val and Earl finally maneuvered the hose into position and moved over to the septic pump's engine. Earl tugged a rag from his back pocket and wiped grease and grime off its pull cord.

"You realize," Earl started, more annoyed with himself than anything else. "Not having a real plan in place is what keeps us doing jobs like this? This week to week shit just keeps us in… shit."

He yanked the cord, and the engine coughed to life.

"No, what keeps us doing jobs like this is you dragging your feet," Val retorted as he slammed open the suction valve.

The hose immediately started to shudder with the pull of vacuum, sucking out all the waste from the cesspool.

Earl glared at him. "You gonna stand there in broad daylight and tell me *I'm* the reason we're still stuck in

Perfection? You wanna know how close I am to leaving right now, do you?"

Val didn't blink. "I'll call that little bluff. How close are you?"

A sharp *POP*, a splintered *POW*, and then the intake hose ruptured as it exploded in a wet, horrifying spray. The contents of the cesspool shot up and out, showering both in a foul, lumpy, rancid rain of waste.

The two staggered back, gagging, swearing, slipping and stumbling in the human mud.

Melvin, far from the shower, laughed so hard he nearly fell out of his chair.

Now covered in filth, soaked to the skin with something they'd rather not think about, Val and Earl looked at each other.

That was it.

They were now done.

They had to go. Now. Enough was enough. And this was more than enough shit for them to stand. Literally and figuratively. Nestor's fifty bucks be damned.

By mid-afternoon, Val and Earl's beat-up trailer was a flurry of chaotic packing. Their place sat just down the street from Walter's store and was a rusted mobile home that barely survived when desert storms hit the area. Now it was finally being evacuated.

Val marched out of the door with a small portable TV under one arm and a framed Coors beer sign under the other. Earl followed, tugging down the clothesline and dumping it, along with the attached shirts, socks, and all, straight into the back of the truck. One that was already piled high with the rest of their worldly possessions.

They were dressed in what they would call their 'best' clothes. But their scale had a very low bar. Their best was just the least dirty or frayed of outfits.

For a moment, as the door closed behind them, they stood staring at each other.

They were serious.

They were resolute.

Without another thought, they got into the truck.

As Val switched the engine to life, he leaned out and casually plucked the old wooden nameplate off their battered mailbox: *E. Basset & V. McKee.*

They drove down the track that cut through Perfection and headed to the mountains, in the direction of whatever waited beyond.

They were *finally* leaving.

Nancy Sterngood came rushing out onto her front porch, waving both arms over her head as Val and Earl's truck drove down the dusty street toward her. Her home was easy to spot among the others that surrounded her. Hers had hand-thrown pottery decorating every inch of the porch and yard. Each with bright glazes flashing in the sunlight like little signal fires.

Seeing her flagging them down, Val reluctantly slowed and rolled down the window. He threw up his hand before Nancy could even open her mouth to greet them.

"Sorry, Nancy. We're not delivering firewood no more," he said. "We're headed for Bixby. Permanently."

A skeptical look crossed her face. Then she saw the truck bed, crammed with their belongings.

Her mouth fell open. "Oh my God, you're not joking," she said, stunned. "You really *are* going this time."

Behind her, Nancy's nine-year-old daughter Mindy came bouncing along on her pogo stick. Her headphones were clamped over her ears. With music from her Walkman playing so loud, Val and Earl could hear its tinny tune from where they sat… even with their engine on. She circled the truck obviously… *bounce, bounce, bounce…* pogoing in rhythm without missing a beat.

"Mindy, honey," Nancy called out loudly, "can't we cool it with the damn pogo stick?"

Mindy was lost in her music and didn't hear her mother.

Earl leaned out the window, raising his voice louder. "Hey, Mindy, what's the count?"

Mindy didn't even look up. "Six hundred three," she said, still bouncing steadily. "Six hundred four… Six hundred five."

Nancy lowered her voice, with a more serious edge. "Please, guys, listen. It isn't firewood I want. I got that big order, remember? I need a new pottery kiln built.

It'd be at *least* a month's work for both of you… I'll even throw in lunches… and beers."

Val and Earl hesitated, glancing at each other. A month's steady work… in Perfection? That was almost unheard of. It was tempting…

…more than tempting…

But…

Earl firmly shook his head. Val nodded in agreement.

Not this time.

As Mindy's bouncing, along with Nancy's hopeful expression, shrank from them in the rearview mirror, the truck drove out of Perfection.

They grinned like they'd just won the lottery.

"We did it!" Earl crowed, thumping the dashboard. "We faced temptation, and we did not bend! Like the devil throwing one more try to keep us here, we faced it down and said. 'Screw you, Satan!'"

"Damn straight!" Val shouted, high on the same victory fumes. "Now there's nothing between us and Bixby except sand and rock… And what else? So long, damn pothole."

On cue, the truck bumped over a hole in the road, half throwing them out of their seats as they laughed.

"Adios, sign!" Earl added as they flew past the hand-painted *Leaving Perfection* sign.

"So long, town!" Val added, as the houses disappeared into a smudge in the distance.

· · ·

The empty, arid desert soon opened up, and the road became awash with shimmering heat waves. Val and Earl in their truck were merely a little metal speck in an endless sea of emptiness.

But soon, the expanse ended and the canyon road began, where the terrain turned jagged and winding. They drove up through narrow rock that loomed up on either side.

"Last time down this twisty ass road!" Val laughed.

But Earl did not. He furrowed his brow as he stared out of the window at what was coming up. "Look at those poor bastards," he said.

Partway down the road, a highway maintenance truck was parked on the shoulder. Two workers were fixing a damaged section where a rockslide had smashed part of the concrete road below.

One of the workers, Carmine, was pounding at the broken asphalt with a jackhammer. The other, Howard, leaned on a shovel nearby, watching without much enthusiasm, as the humidity flooded the canyon around them.

Rolling past, Val slowed just enough to toss Howard a couple of cold beers through the window.

"Hey, guys, drink up!" he yelled. "It's party time!"

Howard caught the beers with a surprised look. Earl and Val drove away without another word, steering around Carmine and the rocks, leaving the canyon walls reverberating with the rumble of their vehicle.

Carmine looked up, and despite the confusion as to how or why, smiled as he saw the beers and stopped his jackhammer. He turned to look at the truck driving away, then back to Howard, who was already twisting off the bottle caps.

"Guess angels come in all shapes and sizes, huh?" he said.

Out the other side of the canyon, Val and Earl had not finished saying their goodbyes quite yet. Their old pickup tore out past a lone mailbox at the end of a long driveway to a shack.

Without even thinking, Val and Earl rolled up their windows at the same time.

A moment later, the reason appeared.

A ferocious dog, all teeth and rage, came barreling down the driveway in hot pursuit. Earl stuck his arm up out of the sunroof and flipped the dog the finger.

"Last chance, asshole," he said with a grin, watching the mutt fall behind as they drove on. "Run, run…!"

At the next shack along the road, Fred Green was at the far end of his large vegetable garden, latching the gate closed on a restless flock of sheep. He looked up just in time to catch sight of Val and Earl's truck hurtling past. They leaned on the horn and waved, laughing, and Fred raised a hand in return, not knowing why they were so happy.

· · ·

The road stretched on, as it began to run parallel to a line of high-tension electrical towers. The truck rattled along at a good clip, as the landscape zoomed by in a dusty blur—nothing but scrub brush and dry rock all the way to the horizon. All the way to Bixby.

Inside the cab, the excitement had worn a little, as Earl, still riding high on dreams of a new life, was talking practically about what would happen next.

"Okay, here's the plan," he said, tapping the dashboard like it was a blueprint. "We bust our tails in the car wash for six months... well, maybe nine... and we don't spend a dime, you know? Just the essentials…"

"Food, beer and smokes," Val added.

"Exactly! Then we go for it, down payment on a tow truck or a backhoe or something. Start a *real* business. Not this Podunk shit we've been peddlin'. We get real gear. Hell, we even get branded shirts with our names on."

Val nodded pointing ahead. "As long as we don't end up doing shit like that guy."

Off in the distance, near the top of one of the massive electrical towers, a figure sat in the criss-crossing steel girders.

Earl gave a grim shake of his head. "Now that's a job I'd never sign up for. Working around electricity is a death sentence. Climbin' them towers, runnin' lines? Hell no. You know that I read it kills fifty men a year for every hundred thousand doin' it. That's a worse statistic than being a cop, worse than oil rigs. No thank you, sir. I'll stick to mending stuff on the ground."

"I'm fine with the electricity, it's the damn height that gets me," Val added.

As they drew closer, something about the figure made Val's smile suddenly fade.

"Hey, hold up a sec…" he said, sitting up straighter. "Ain't that Edgar Deems?"

"Oh, come on," Earl said impatiently. "What would an old fart like Edgar be doing fifty feet up a pole? It's just a linesman."

"No, I'm telling you. He only wears that one damn jacket, right? That's *him*."

Earl eased the truck to the side of the road and killed the engine.

Together they climbed out, craning their necks to the figure perched halfway up the large buzzing tower.

It was tough to tell through all the crossing beams, but the figure was definitely Edgar. He was strapped to the structure by his belt, his Winchester rifle still gripped tightly in his hands.

"Is that a rifle?" Val asked quietly.

Earl gave a low whistle. "Man, oh man. He must've really been drunk this time." He cupped his hands around his mouth and shouted up, "Hey Edgar! What the hell are you doing? Get on down from there before you hurt yer'self, you old bastard!"

Edgar didn't move. Didn't flinch. Didn't even turn his head.

Val and Earl exchanged a silent uneasy look.

Finally, Val sighed.

"Well, shit," he said.

"This can't be good," Earl added, dreading the worst.

"We can't just leave him up there, all drunk and asleep. He'll be cooked by sundown."

They both knew what was coming next.

Without a word, they raised their fists for the Challenge. Rock, paper, scissors… quick, silent, decisive.

Earl had rock.

Val had scissors.

Val lost.

"Thank you, Edgar, ya old coot," he said bitterly. He reached into the back of the truck, picked out a pair of leather worker gloves and walked over to the tower.

Even with those gloves, the steel was hot under Val's palms. Far too hot. But he carried on anyway, trying not to look down as he climbed higher and higher.

"Hey, Edgar," he called out, his voice echoing off the surrounding metal. "Don't you move. I'm coming to get you, okay? You damn booze hound, you owe me big on this one…"

As he climbed closer, a swarm of flies buzzed thickly in the air. Surrounding Edgar as he slumped against a girder. Val edged carefully around the beams until he could get a look at Edgar's face. Expecting to find him passed out in a stupor.

But this was no stupor.

Edgar's eyes were open. Wide open. Milky, blank and unfocused.

"What the hell?" Val gasped.

Edgar was stone cold dead.

Fred Green was still in his vegetable patch, methodically hoeing the soil among the rows of carrots. He glanced up as he heard a truck's engine, and saw Val and Earl speeding back at incredible speed, back to Perfection.

At the next shack along the road, even the asshole dog didn't have time to get up and chase after them.

Jim and Megan's house sat a mile before town, an ongoing project caught somewhere between a dream and ambition. And it had been stuck like that for over a year.

A big old station wagon, along with a small trailer, rested in the shade of a skeletal house-in-progress; half-complete walls, framed in lumber.

Jim and Megan Wallace had retired to Perfection, with the intent of building their dream home. But it wasn't unfinished due to laziness or lack of money. They were the kind of people who always found new projects to take on, which kept delaying the build more and more.

Val and Earl's truck sat in front of the trailer. In its bed, on top of all their belongings, lay the body of Edgar Deems, dead and sunbaked. His boots pointed stiffly to the sky.

Jim leaned in the truck, with his sleeves rolled up and a look of concern on his face as he examined Edgar. Val and Earl stood with Megan to one side.

Val spoke, his Stetson in hand, his voice low and respectful. "We're real sorry to bother you with this, Megan," he said. "But we didn't know what else to do. We figured since Jim's a doctor and all…"

Megan nodded with a comforting smile. "No, it's fine. You did the right thing," she said. "When Jim's done, we'll call the coroners in Bixby. We'll take care of it all, don't you worry." Her gaze lingered on Edgar. "Poor old man," she added softly, shaking her head. "Not a good way to go."

Earl, ever the one to dodge discomfort with small talk, tried to shift the mood. He nodded at the skeletal house behind her.

"Well, I see you got all the framing up at last."

Megan managed a half-smile. "Greenhouse was done, so guess we had to get back to the house. Besides, the frame was the easy part. You two did the foundation. That was the real hard labor! And I gotta say, I'm sure sorry that you're leaving… And this ain't a good last memory of Perfection is it?"

Before they could respond, Jim stepped down from the tailgate, brushing his hands off, with a sad look on his face.

"It was a heart attack, right?" Earl asked.

Jim shook his head slowly. "That would have been a much better way to go… No, he died of dehydration. Thirst."

Val looked confused. "But that doesn't make sense. That takes a couple of days, doesn't it? You can go a few without water."

"Three to five, even," Jim replied. "Depending on all the conditions. In this heat, at his age? It's tough to pinpoint."

Earl stared down to the ground, trying to wrap his head around the words. "You mean he sat up there for the best part of a week? Just stayed 'til he died? Didn't think once to get down?"

Jim couldn't offer any answers. He didn't have any. He just stood there, helpless in the face of the uncertainty.

The group stood for a moment in uneasy silence.

"But why did he have his gun?" Val asked, adding to their confusion.

Fred was still hoeing.

As he raked at the earth, inside the pen behind him, his sheep paced nervously, bumping into one another with muted bleats. Fred glanced at them, frowning slightly, as he wondered once more what could be spooking them so much. There were no coyotes, cougars, bobcats or anything resembling a threat around. With a shrug he went back to his work, resigning himself to the fact the sheep were just playing up out of boredom.

Behind him, something moved under the cabbage rows.

The scarecrow, standing stiffly between the rows, wavered slightly in the wind, or at least it appeared to. But there was no breeze today, and no reason for it to tilt at all.

Unaware, Fred kept hoeing, humming under his breath.

As a low, muffled sound rose from the ground beneath, catching his attention, he slowly stopped and looked around.

The sheep in the pen were bleating louder and more raucously than before.

Something was wrong.

Then, before he could turn back, the ground split in two and something yanked Fred downward. One moment he was there, hoe in hand. The next, he was… gone with a single yelp.

The seismograph needle twitched, tracing frantic jagged lines where a steady reading should be.

Rhonda LeBeck stood next to the machine, brow furrowed, with a geology field manual open in her hand. She flipped pages, determined to figure out why the machines kept malfunctioning and giving the craziest readings. With a frustrated sigh, she resorted to the last-ditch attempt to fix the machine. She kicked the casing. But the needle kept on jumping, registering something underground. But she could not feel the ground shaking. Today was as still as it always was.

· · ·

Val and Earl sat in a morose silence as they drove Bixby-bound once again. Ahead of them they approached the shack past the canyon for the second time that day. This time, though, they were too caught up to notice that the asshole dog was nowhere to be seen. Not chasing them. Not barking.

Suddenly realizing, Earl slowed, pointing a finger to the shack.

"Where the hell is he?"

Val, suddenly realizing, looked around hurriedly, half expecting the dog to burst through one of their open windows. But there was no sign of the dog anywhere.

"Reckon he hated Perfection as much as us?" Earl said, dryly. "You suppose he *wanted* to kill himself?"

"Why would the dog kill itself?" Val asked.

Earl shot Val a look of contempt. "Not the dog, I'm talking about Edgar!"

Realizing his mistake, Val chuckled, before remembering Edgar up the tower. His dead eyes staring back at him. Val's smile dropped. "You don't climb up high to die like that. Come on. Somebody must've chased him up there."

"Someone? You mean someone who ain't scared of a Winchester rifle," Earl asked. "And then what'd they do? Camp out below and just wait for him to die? For days? He would have filled 'em full of lead. The gun was fully loaded! Nah, something else is up."

Val shrugged. "Maybe he wasn't thinking straight? My Gramma had that mind thing. Where she forgot where she was and who she was. He could have had that?"

"Dementia?" Earl pondered this surprisingly plausible theory. "Well, that actually makes a hell of a lot more sense than suicide, or someone chasing him up there."

It was all too weird, too far outside anything that made sense for either of them to truly comprehend.

They drove on.

"Okay, so we just get to Bixby," Val added. "No more stops 'til we're—"

Earl suddenly skidded the truck, tires throwing up a spray of loose gravel as he stared out at Fred's place.

"What the hell ya doin?" Val asked, startled as Earl stared wide-eyed out the window.

He followed Earl's gaze, then he saw it too. He felt his stomach drop at the sight.

The sheep pen was empty. Not a single bleating, woolly body remained. The ground inside the fence was dug up, torn and messy in large piles that could be seen above the wire fencing. Tufts of bloody wool littered the areas.

Without needing to talk about it, both men bolted out of the truck and toward the house.

"Hey, Fred? You here?" Earl shouted rushing inside the shack. "Fred? Where are you? What happened to your sheep?"

Outside, Val circled the vegetable garden and the pen, looking around with a sense of growing dread, seeing all the bloody chunks laying in the ripped-up earth.

Earl came back out, shaking his head. "Not here… He left the door open, radio on. Kettle boiling on the stove."

That's when Val spotted something lying a few yards away, half-buried among the carrot rows. It was Fred's old, battered wide brim hat.

Still looking around, Val ambled over and crouched to pick the hat up. As he did, he peered down and recoiled with a strangled yell. Earl made the same noise as his hands flew to his mouth.

Fred was still wearing his hat.

His mangled body was somewhere else, deep in the dirt, with only his head there, frozen in a horrified scream, eyes wide. Blood and torn flesh crawled out of the dirt and up to his neck, stopping just short of his ears.

"Oh, Jesus!" Earl said.

Val staggered, shaking his head like he could will the image away.

"What the hell is going on?" Val shouted. "I mean, what the *hell* is going on?"

Down the canyon road, Carmine and Howard continued their work, slowly repairing the cracked road. Carmine's jackhammer rattled and clanged, while Howard stood to one side like before, half-watching, half-bored. The two beer bottles they had been given were long drunk, and any effects that may have brought with them were long dissipated.

Approaching fast, Val drove the truck back through the canyon pass and skidded to a stop in front of them.

Earl leaned out the passenger side window, waving his arms to get Howard's attention.

"Hey," Howard said as he recognized them, shouting over the sound of the Jackhammer. "Thanks for the brewskis, man. Much appreciated."

Earl ignored the thanks and just called back. "You guys better get the hell outta here!" he shouted. "We got a killer on the loose!" But his words were garbled over the noise.

Howard waved at Carmine to cut the jackhammer, unsure of what he was just saying.

Carmine nodded and let the machine rattle to a stop.

"What did you say?" Howard asked, clearer now.

"A murderer, man!" Earl replied. "A real psycho! He's cut off someone's head! I'm serious! I'd high-tail it far out of here if I were you. Or get the hell back into town."

Before the workers could think of a reply, Val gunned the gas pedal and the truck sped off, leaving the workmen confused.

Howard shook his head. "They're pullin' our chains, right?"

"Yeah," Carmine agreed with a disapproving smirk, turning back to his work. "Bunch of cowboys if you ask me."

He fired the jackhammer up again, and as the machine pounded into the broken road, as the bit sunk below the road, something immediately happened.

There should have been compacted earth, but instead the rod struck something much softer. Something that shouldn't have been there.

As it cut in, a piercing, unearthly shriek sounded from under his feet. A noise that sounded like metal scraping across bone. And as it sounded, a strangely fluorescent orange goo burst upward, around the hole, splattering across Carmine's boots.

The stench was instant and terrible.

Before Carmine could move, the jackhammer was suddenly yanked sideways from under the road, and as it did, it dragged him along with it.

He screamed, as he then became tangled in the writhing air hose. The jackhammer crunching across the road, tearing through the solid road, pulling him along like a hooked fish.

The air hose ripped clean off the nearby compressor, making a loud *POP!*

"Help!" was all Carmine could cry out.

Howard grabbed a crowbar and ran after the jackhammer as it ripped across the road at dizzying speed and surged up the edge of the high embankment.

All Howard could see as he tried to catch up was the torn end of the flapping air hose disappearing over the top, and the sound of Carmine's screams faded.

"Hey!" he shouted, scrambling up after him. "Are you okay?!"

A light shower of muck and pebbles rattled down the embankment toward him. But it was the sudden deep rumble that made Howard freeze.

In that split second, Howard could tell what was coming, but he had no idea how.

The ground above let out a deep, groaning crack, and the hillside above the embankment began to fall. A wall of mud and rock came crashing down and with that, Howard was gone.

CHAPTER 3

SNAKES OR ALIENS

Inside the store, Walter leaned on the counter, deep in conversation with Miguel, one of the local ranchers. An old radio played quietly beside them, filling the room with the drone of a barely audible country song.

Both men jumped as the front doors banged open and Val and Earl burst in, covered in dirt and panic. Behind them, Nestor and Melvin trailing behind. Without missing a step, Val and Earl made a beeline for the payphone on the far wall.

Melvin, sounding almost excited, was in the middle of finding out what happened. "You serious? Old Fred? They cut off his *head?* Are you bullshitting me, Val. C'mon! That true?"

Val didn't answer. He took the receiver off the wall and searched his pockets for a quarter, but found none. He only had a lighter, an old scrap of paper and a broken toothpick. Earl, meanwhile, had already fished out a handful of change and slapped a few coins into Val's hand.

Walter looked with concern. "Did you say that something happen to Old Fred?"

Earl nodded. "Yeah. And a lot worse than what happened to Edgar."

"Wait, what?" Miguel straightened up. "What happened to Edgar?"

Val punched the buttons on the payphone, but after a few clicks and a hollow silence, nothing happened. He slammed the receiver back onto the hook and turned, exasperated.

"I don't believe this! The phone's out!" He turned and pointed at Walter. "Hey, your phone is out!"

"Well, I didn't do it!" Walter threw up his hands. "So, you gonna say what's going on? And who'd you need to call so bad?"

But Val and Earl didn't stick around to explain. They turned and headed back out the door to their truck. Everyone else followed.

Val was now behind the wheel, looking for the key in his pocket.

"We've gotta get the police up here!" Nestor shouted. "You guys gotta step on it to Bixby!"

Earl took the truck key from his shirt pocket and handed it to Val.

"Consider it stepped on." Val replied, jamming the key into the ignition.

Once again, the truck tore through the narrow canyon, rattling dangerously fast over the uneven and winding ground.

Val gripped the wheel, eyes focused ahead.

"Man," he said, "we decided to leave this place just one day too late, you know?"

Earl sat slumped in the passenger seat looking defeated. "Well, there's sure as hell nothing to stop us now," he said. "Everybody we know between here and Bixby is already dead. I can't—"

He stopped in his tracks. "*Look out!*"

Val slammed the brakes. The truck slid sideways, tires screaming against the sandy road.

Just ahead, their path out of the canyon had gone. Consumed by a massive rockslide that completely buried it, filling up the narrow road. An uprooted telephone pole stood at an angle across the heap like the cherry on the cake, having been dragged down from the top of the embankment.

In shock, they stared, trying to figure out what could possibly be happening.

Earl was dumbfounded, getting angrier and more resentful by the second. "Is there some higher force at work here? Are we asking too much of life? *Is some almighty sonofabitch sittin' on a cloud, messin' with us for fun?*"

But Val wasn't in the mood for anger. He jumped out of the truck, and moved to the abandoned highway maintenance truck sitting off the side of the road. Its emergency lights still flashed, rotating silently, as if the workers were there… but there was no sign of Carmine nor Howard.

Val looked around, at their level and high up. "What the hell are you doing? Blasting?" he yelled. "Hey, where are you guys? It's not like there's another road, assholes!"

As he walked forward, Earl hissed from behind, pointing urgently at the ground "Val. *Val!*"

Val turned, then saw it.

At the edge of the landslide, Howard's hardhat lay on the dirt, smeared with blood.

All at once, the real danger smashed into clear and undeniable focus.

"Pick it up!" Earl called over.

"Nope, screw that, not doin' that again," Val said as he raced back to the truck. "I ain't wanting to see another head." Opening the door, he thrust his hand under the driver's seat until he found a battered box of bullets.

But when he reached for the revolver in the glove box, Earl was already there, having taken it.

Val shoved the box of bullets into Earl's hands and got into the truck. He turned the key and the truck coughed to life once more, rumbling hoarsely, as if it were complaining that it had been used too much already.

Earl put six bullets into the revolver as fast as his fingers could work.

Val threw the truck into reverse, slamming his foot on the gas, but as the truck rocked back a couple of yards, there was a sharp clunk from underneath. Their path out stalled.

He moved the gear stick back into first, but as he did, the engine whined.

The truck wasn't moving.

"Jesus! I don't *believe* this!" Val shouted, slamming his palm against the steering wheel.

"You gotta be hung up on something," Earl said, leaning out the window to look down at the ground. "Maybe some rock or wire got ya."

"I'm not hung up on shit!"

Despite doubting, Val then leaned out his side to double check. The rear tires were clear. No rocks, no cables. Nothing that could hold them.

"See nothing," he said.

"Nope, not here either," Earl replied, checking his side.

Val tried to ease forward. The truck rocked again, as something held them from going in any direction. Smoke began to rise from around the gear stick as the engine whined loudly.

"You *gotta* be hung up on something, what else could it be," Earl said as he warned, "slow it, you're gonna burn out the clutch!"

But Val wasn't having it. Desperate to get them out of here, he slammed the truck into a low-range four-wheel-drive and floored the gas in reverse. As he did, the tires bit in deep, gravel spraying everywhere.

It took a few seconds of wheel spinning, but finally, with a jarring lurch, the truck broke free. As it did, a squelching sound was heard as an eerie shriek rose from beneath the loud growl of the engine.

Neither of them had any intention to hang around and find out what made that sound.

He spun the car around as fast as he could, and drove back to town at maximum speed.

"Jesus, you could have broken an axle like that!" Earl said, having braced himself against the dash.

"Could you shut up, Earl?!" Val barked.

"Hey, I don't need to spend the night out here 'cause you got all stupid!"

By the time they screeched to a stop outside Walter's, half the town was already waiting for them. Word had already spread. Burt Gummer was at the front of the crowd, a huge rifle slung over one shoulder, as he wore yellow-tinted shooting glasses.

"What the hell are you two doing back here already?" Burt demanded. "What about Bixby? The police?"

Val got out of the truck. "You're never gonna believe this," he said, gesturing wildly. "The canyon road... we were just on it an hour ago... well, *now* it's completely—"

He stopped talking as soon as he realized that no one was listening or even looking at him. They were all staring in confusion at the truck.

Val and Earl turned to see too, and their jaws dropped.

Hanging from the rear axle, trailing along the ground like some gory wedding train, was a six-foot-long grotesque line of meat. It was slick with orange goo and very fleshy. The end where it wrapped around the axle looked horrifying, ringed at the tip with four sharp, bony spikes that protruded from it. It was ragged and torn from being dragged across the road, as the goo oozed down onto the dirt around it.

Viola stood at the back, holding her gargoyle dog, who yapped away at anything it could.

"That's unreal!" Melvin smiled. "Where'd you get it?"

Val looked stunned at the monstrous appendage. "Uh… I didn't know we had it."

"That's just disgusting, *whatever* it is," Nancy exclaimed, sickened, covering her mouth.

"Maybe it's some kind of snake?" Val guessed weakly.

Miguel knelt for a closer look. "Looks more like… an eel."

"But… eels live in water," Nestor said, confused. "Don't they?"

"Bigger than a damn eel," Earl said. "Maybe a big mother slug."

Burt, more curious than afraid, fetched a shovel from the truck bed and immediately went to prying the thing off the axle. Not a single drop of sweat was broken as he grunted, working the shovel, and the snake thing soon slopped to the ground.

Walter hovered nearby, wringing his hands, staring at it. "Don't touch! Don't touch!"

"Relax," Burt said coolly. "It's dead."

Viola walked forward, yapping dog in hand.

Hearing this, Earl shot her a look. "Keep that monster away from me, Viola!"

Everyone stopped. Looked at the yapping dog, then to the thing.

Earl noticed everyone then stared at him. "Small dogs creep me out, okay? Anyway, we got more pressing matters." He nudged Val as he nodded to the snake thing. "It must've grabbed us. That's why the truck stalled?"

"Okay fine, I was hung up! You win!"

Earl wanted to say *I told you so* but thought better of it.

Burt moved the long slimy snake out from under the truck, and laid it on the ground in front of them. Turning it over with the shovel, he inspected it thoughtfully. "This stalled out your truck? Have to have been one strong son of a gun. Was there any more to it?"

"We weren't sticking around to find out," Earl replied.

Walter suddenly darted forward, a gleam in his eye. "I'll give you boys five dollars for the snake."

Val and Earl squared their shoulders toward him. This time, they weren't going to be taken for suckers.

"How about twenty?" Val said.

"Okay, you win, ten dollars it is," Walter countered immediately. "Cold hard cash."

"Fifteen," Earl cut in.

Walter didn't hesitate. "Okay, fifteen. I give in."

"Damn right, fifteen," Val said, crossing his arms.

As the deal was struck, Burt was still crouched beside the shredded thing, frowning in thought.

"Might be a snake," he said. "Some kind of mutation. But whatever it is…" He shook his head. "Just one of these couldn't have eaten Fred. Or Edgar. Or his whole flock of sheep." He motioned to the torn end. "There has gotta be more to it. Who knows how long it could be."

"Or that got ruined just being dragged?" Miguel said.

"Could it be an elephant trunk?" Viola asked, as her dog shouted a chorus of yaps around her.

No one replied to that suggestion.

Burt stood up, grabbed the rifle from his shoulder and surveyed the desert stretching out beyond the town. He was ready for a fight.

"My guess is there's more than one." He gritted his teeth. "There's a lot more of them out there."

A nervous silence fell over the group. Not all of them were as willing as Burt. Slowly, they all turned to look out at the vast desert surrounding Perfection.

.   .   .

Rhonda picked up her hat from the desert floor and put it on, unaware of the danger now facing the residents of Perfection.

The valley she had wandered into was blisteringly hot, much more so than the open plains she had just worked in. Here, it felt like an oven. Wiping her brow, she drove a marking stake into the dirt near one of the seismographs. With each hammer strike, the needle jumped, responding exactly as expected.

When she paused, so did the needle. She exhaled, confused. The machines, which had been acting erratically earlier, now seemed to be functioning perfectly.

She fetched another stake from the back of her truck, unaware that the needle twitched again, this time without her touching anything.

As she hammered in the second stake a few feet away, she looked over and saw the needle flicker once more. She frowned, assuming it was just her movements, but she wasn't the only thing causing the ground to stir.

There was something else. Something that was far away, and had quickened its pace toward her.

As it passed through a small burrow that hid under the surface, a rabbit shot out from a patch of undergrowth, streaking away across the valley floor twenty yards away, catching Rhonda's eye, as she was now pounding in a third stake.

Rhonda's seismograph gave a sudden tilt, as the dirt

underneath bulged out, almost imperceptibly, disturbing the heavy device.

Finishing her pounding of the third stake, Rhonda had no idea what was coming. She was too busy grumbling under her breath, giving up. She picked up the shovels and field tools she had lying around and took them back over to the truck, throwing them in the back, then slamming the tailgate shut with a loud metallic slam.

Rhonda was now ready to pack it all in, and not just for the day. She could not work out here with the machines showing such erratic results with no cause.

She got into the driver's seat of her truck, but just as she did, the cause appeared. The ground split open just ahead of the truck, and a fleshy, muscular snake-like creature thrust out. At its tip, a beak-like mouth groped at the empty space where her boots had just been a second earlier. Slashing through the air blindly, missing her by a matter of seconds. Not that Rhonda had a clue.

She turned on the engine without paying any attention, and switched the radio on loudly. The truck bounced as it rolled forward, the tires unknowingly crushing the beaked creature flat to the dirt. A shriek of pain spread throughout the ground, but Rhonda was too busy loudly singing along to the song on the radio to notice. Forcing herself to ignore her failures today but singing at the top of her lungs.

· · ·

That night, as the sun took most of the heat with it, the mood in the store was now a strange one; a mix of tension, confusion and absurdity. Everyone was still there.

Mindy Sterngood was posed cautiously beside the grotesque creature that had been proudly mounted on a makeshift display stand, her smile forced yet determined. A bright camera flash lit her face as Walter took a photo on a Polaroid camera. A sign beside them read in large pen-written letters: *Photographs: You and the Snake Monster - $3.00.*

The rest of the people here all spoke in low, worried voices. Talking about what they should do next, about how they could defend themselves, and just what the hell it was that they were dealing with. Near the back, Val and Earl leaned against the bar, sipping cold beers and watching Walter's enterprise with stunned admiration.

"Slick as snot and I'm not lying," Earl said, shaking his head.

"Fifteen lousy bucks though. Are we stupid?"

"It's not that. *He* is a man who plans ahead," Earl replied. "We should be more like that."

The town's discussion was dominated by Burt and Heather Gummer, both armed to the teeth with scoped hunting rifles, holstered Magnum's revolvers, and various blades strapped to their belts. Heather stood at the window, peering into the darkness outside. Viola was sat on a chair, her gargoyle dog still yapping every few seconds.

Burt was busy addressing the small yet anxious crowd. "Look, we organize, we arm ourselves. We take turns standing guard. Standard military procedure is key. If those damn snake things come around here, we make 'em extinct with extreme prejudice."

"All right!" Melvin whooped from the back.

Nestor frowned. "Come on, Burt. We don't even know what these things are or even if they did that to Edgar and Fred."

Miguel added, "Yeah, you make it sound like a war, when we have no idea."

Mindy skipped over, staring happily at her new photograph. "Could be aliens," she said. "They sure look freaky deaky."

"Why are we even looking for trouble?" Miguel added. "You're presuming a hell of a lot from nothing at all. So what, they found that snake thing on their truck? Did anyone see it attack? No. You're all jumping to conclusions.

"What have you people got against being prepared?" Burt said exasperated. He turned to Miguel. "Look, you have it backward. We are not looking to fight snakes. We are preparing *in case*. We haven't gone looking for trouble, the trouble's come to us. And if we're not ready…"

Nancy, arms across her chest, cut in sharply. "Wait a minute. Walter's got a radio. Why aren't you calling somebody in Bixby? The police or—?"

"Call in those Navy Seals!" Viola suggested.

Everyone ignored her suggestion again.

"That can't reach outside the valley," Walter cut in. "You know, because of the mountains?"

Heather spoke from the window, never taking her eyes off the darkness. "Phone's out. Road's out. We're on our own here, people."

Nancy snorted. "And you two just love it, don't you?"

Heather turned, frowning. "Come on, Nancy. Don't let's get personal. We need to *do* something."

"This is crazy," Miguel said, clearly not buying into the plan. "It was one snake you found!"

Burt stepped over to the faded topographic map of the area that was pinned to the wall. He tapped it, pointing out the facts. "You all gotta analyze the situation. With that road out, we're completely cut off. Got the cliffs to the north, mountains east and west. That's why Heather and me settled here in the first place. Geographic isolation."

Nancy chewed her lip, thinking hard, and it clearly took a lot of willpower. "Well... there must be *some* way to get help."

"We're not on the moon, for God's sake," Nestor said. "Bixby's not *that* far."

"How you gonna do that then?" Burt turned to face them all. "You gonna walk thirty-eight miles to Bixby across open desert?"

"What about Walter's saddle horses?" Nestor replied.

Every head in the store swiveled to Walter expectantly.

Walter, caught off-guard, sighed. "Fine… You're welcome to them," he said.

Nestor nodded. "Somebody could ride to Bixby."

Miguel didn't look any more convinced but knew that his opinion was holding no sway here.

Burt nodded. "Horses? That's not a bad idea at all. Who's best riding here?"

The whole crowd then slowly turned to Val and Earl, who were still sipping their beers, examining the topographic map, not really listening to what was being said.

Feeling the weight of a dozen stares, they both turned to the crowd at the same time, looking around without any clue.

"Aw shit, what we gotta do now?" Earl moaned.

Far out in the desert, Jim and Megan Wallace's half-finished house sat in the glare of a harsh white floodlight. One that cut through the house's dark shell, and onto their nearby station wagon.

The soft hum of country music drifted from the car's radio, as Jim and Megan, dusty and exhausted, were in the middle of hauling bundles of roofing shingles to the house.

Jim grunted as he tried lifting another heavy stack, but soon gave up, sinking the pile back onto the tailgate with an exhausted wheeze. "I'm *done…* I retired so I could take it easy. Can't we just stop for a while?"

"Well, what do you wanna do?" Megan asked.

"Let's just finish all this in the morning, huh?"

Megan placed her bundle of shingle on the ground. "The morning?" she said. "We have to go into Bixby in the morning… The cinder blocks are in."

Jim groaned. "The cinderblocks? Oh my God… More damn heavy lifting? Damn you Earl! Damn you Val!"

Megan laughed, stretching her back. "We just gotta keep on going, looking at that beautiful night sky."

Jim looked at her with a raised eyebrow. "What now?"

"That's the sky that's gonna be over *our* roof every night when we're done," she said warmly. "Just gotta keep remembering why we did this and push through."

"Ah, but consider this—if we don't finish the roof, we can look at that sky *all the time.*"

Megan laughed again, but as she did the generator's soft hum faltered, and the noise suddenly ran down to a stop. The floodlight illuminating them soon began to flicker, then cut out. They were immediately plunged into darkness. Only the distant, oddly cheerful music from the radio could be heard and, beyond what was lit by the stars and moon, the only light still working was the glow from the dashboard.

"Damn that thing," Jim said, grabbing a flashlight from the trunk of the car behind him.

"We could always buy a new generator," Megan said. "One that isn't a rickety box of rusty bolts."

"Walter said it was top of the line!"

Megan laughed. "And you believed him?"

Jim switched on the flashlight and walked over to where the generator was.

He soon stopped in his tracks.

"What in carnations," he mumbled. "It was right there… Wasn't it??"

Megan hurried to his side, taking the flashlight from his hand, convinced he was just being a joker. She swept the beam across the dirt.

All that was there was the heavy electric cord, severed, ending at a cone-shaped depression in the earth.

"You sure you didn't move it?" she asked.

"It was right *here*," Jim said, pointing. "Look, there's the damn cable for it."

He knelt to examine the loose dirt. Megan grabbed his shirt, trying to pull him back.

"Well don't!" she said. "Looks like the ground gave way there… You don't wanna fall in… Gotta be a sinkhole or something."

"Maybe," he thought aloud. "There's a lot of old mines and stuff around here. Ground is more or less like Swiss cheese, it's got so many holes."

Suddenly, with a massive *WHOOMP*, the generator burst out of the ground ten yards away, flying through the air and crashing down with a thunderous noise. The whole thing was crushed, twisted, bent out of recognizable shape, and covered in a glistening slime.

Jim stared, too transfixed in disbelief to have jumped in shock.

But Megan was full of enough worry for the both of them. "Come on! Get away from it!"

At that moment, the smell of the slime covering the crushed generator reached them.

"Sweet Jesus, what *is* that stink?" Jim asked.

A low rumble then began to be felt through their feet, making them both suddenly look at each other in a panic.

"Never mind! Let's just *go*!" Megan begged. "Let's drive into town or something, Jim, *please*!"

As they got up and hurried to the car, Jim kept talking as she dragged him along by the arm. "You know, I bet it's geological or something. Like natural gas. Or a geyser. They smell bad like that. Remember in Yellowstone—"

His words cut off with his own pained scream, as he was pulled downward, up to the waist in the dirt in a fraction of a second.

"Something's got my leg!!" he yelled.

Megan cried out as she ran over to him.

But his yells turned to terrible screams, as sickening noises came from under the earth. He thrashed wildly, reaching for Megan, unable to get free. His arms clawed at the air, as the pain ripped through his nerves.

"God! Get me out!" he cried out in agony. "Help me, please!"

His struggling and screams did not stop him being pulled down more.

Megan grabbed a nearby two-by-four, and put it on the dirt in front of him to grab hold onto. Jim seized it desperately like a drowning man gripping to a life raft, but the strength of what was pulling him down was too much. The wood immediately splintered inward and snapped like a twig.

Megan grabbed for Jim's arms, but he had sunk too fast out of her reach. His face contorted in panic before the dirt swallowed him whole.

Then there was nothing. No rumble. No screams. Only the sound of the car radio playing music.

For a second Megan sat on the ground stunned, staring at the spot Jim was pulled into, unable to think what she could possibly do.

The ground then erupted around her.

Two grotesque snakes shot out from the earth, narrowly missing her face. She scrambled backward, crying loudly, as she ran as fast as she could toward her station wagon.

She jumped headfirst into the back, slamming its tailgate closed just as a tentacle slashed at the metal.

Without stopping, she tumbled into the front seat.

Thank God… the keys were still in the ignition.

Before she could turn them, she paused.

The rumbling had stopped.

Looking around, all she could hear was the song on the radio. Not knowing what she had done, she felt relief. Maybe those things had—

The snake-like things shot out of the dirt at the back of the car in full force, attacking it in a frenzy. One tire was shredded almost instantly as a pointed creature lashed at it and cut through the rubber as if it were nothing. Another slapped at the window, trying to break through.

Megan turned the ignition and floored the gas, but the ruined tire peeled off its rim, as the naked wheel dug into the loose dirt, trapping the station wagon where it stood.

With no escape, Megan did the only thing she could think of. She locked the doors, rolled up the windows, and crouched in the driver's seat, shaking and sobbing. Unable to think straight. The image of Jim screaming as he was dragged under was burning into her mind. She stared out at the flailing thing in utter abject and confused horror.

Outside, the things now multiplied around the car. They slithered and slashed heavily, taking a grip of anything they could, and shaking the chassis violently.

And then came something worse.

The things suddenly stopped and dropped out of sight.

Seconds passed. Megan started to feel some relief.

Peeking out of the window, with tears streaming from her eyes, she could not help but think that they had given up, that she was safe. That it was over.

Nothing else happened for a few moments as Megan stopped crying and turned back to try and drive the car out of the dirt.

But it was far from over, as the car started to shake and shudder.

The ground underneath it began to heave and sink, heave and sink, like the very earth was breathing. And as it did, the station wagon slowly started to sink down, its rear end falling first.

Megan screamed as she realized what was happening, and she honked the horn again and again, in heavy desperate blasts that were lost among the isolation around her.

Dust soon picked up from the loosening ground and started to swirl around the windows like a cyclone.

The hood jerked upward as the car tilted back into the earth, being pulled inch by each second by second, vanishing under.

"Stop it!" she cried out hopelessly. "Stop it! Somebody please *help*!"

The last thing to disappear was the glow of the headlights, two bright beacons sending their beams skyward through the roiling dust, up into the night sky.

The sounds of her pleading and the music from the radio got fainter, as the headlights sank from view, and the car was completely engulfed.

Deep in the ground, as she faced what lay beneath, Megan's final scream was only heard by something very much not human.

CHAPTER 4

ROADBLOCK

Outside Walter's store, everyone had gathered in the cool dawn air.

There was a nervous energy among them as Val and Earl saddled up a pair of Walter's 'premium horses' as he called them. For Walter though, his premium often meant the cheapest option. These horses were slightly overweight and way beyond their prime. Premium was, without a doubt, relative here.

Walter himself bustled around the horses, stuffing their saddlebags with food and supplies, throwing in extras like everyone's lives might depend on it.

Val eyed the horses skeptically. "Walter, we don't want to be stuck on a couple of canners," he said. "They better be fast."

"Better this horse than no horse, huh?" Walter replied. "As I said, premium!"

"Val, relax," Earl muttered, checking the cinch on

his saddle. "A snake thing like that couldn't move too quick, could it? I mean. I can outrun a rattler."

"Screw that," Val snapped. "For all you know, they could fly. They look like any snakes you've seen before?"

Earl didn't reply. He just walked back over to the truck and reached into the back, pulling out the old Smith & Wesson revolver and Edgar Deems' battered Winchester rifle. He held them up like a game show prize.

"You want the Smith," he asked, "or Edgar's rifle?"

Val didn't even hesitate. "The rifle."

Of course, Earl wanted it too. They both raised their fists automatically. Rock, paper, scissors.

One, two, three.

Earl lost.

He handed over the Winchester to Val and muttered about how unfair it all was.

As they finished prepping their gear, Burt and Heather Gummer rolled up in their camo-painted Blazer, climbing out with rifles still slung across their backs. The survivalist couple looked even more serious than usual, as they scored around them to make sure all was safe along the perimeter.

"You guys all set?" Burt asked.

"Ready as we'll ever be," Earl replied.

"Heather and I are gonna drive around a little," Burt said, racking a fresh magazine into his rifle. "See if we can find that college girl. Tell her to get her ass back into town. Can't have civilians in danger."

"Good idea," Val said. "And we'll swing by the doc's

place. They were headed to Bixby, but we got no idea if they made it out before the canyon road was blocked."

Val and Earl swung into the saddles, the horses shifting under their weight.

Miguel shook his head, still not believing it. "Are you sure this isn't a lot of hoohah for nothin'? You saw one snake… whatever it is. And now you are convinced they are after us and killing people? C'mon, I know I don't know nothing' about nothin' but this seems a bit… OTT."

Burt grunted. "What would you prefer? We do nothing and wait 'til we're proved right? Or do this and make sure we are safe *in case* we're right?"

Miguel had no reply.

"I thought not," Burt smiled, enjoying a tiny victory.

"You can't chance it with a Smith & Wesson," Heather called out. "Those things are child's play." She walked back and reached into the Blazer, and came back with a heavy, serious-looking hunting rifle. "You oughta take something that packs more punch than that. Take one of our Browning autos, or…" She motioned to her own rifle. "…you can take my Model Seventy if it's more your thing." She smiled proudly. "It's three-seventy-five H and H mag, fully custom tuned."

Earl's eyes lit up. He motioned to the Model Seventy, which she gladly handed over.

"Man with taste," she smiled.

Earl shot Val a smug look, before turning back to

her. "Really... Thanks, Heather. But I hope we don't need it."

Heather unhooked a box of cartridges from her belt and handed them to him.

A sudden blood curdling scream pulled their attention to the store, where the doors were barged open.

Melvin ran out, terrified, wrapped head to toe in Walter's captured monster, writhing in apparent agony.

"It's got me! It's got me! Arrrgghhhh!"

Everyone scattered like cattle, and in an instant Burt and Heather whipped up their weapons, training their scopes on Melvin's thrashing body. Chaos erupted, but as soon as it had come, it quickly died out, as Melvin collapsed in the dirt, howling with laughter.

As everyone realized what had happened, their fear did not turn to amusement. Far from it.

Burt stormed over, grabbed Melvin by the collar, and yanked him to his feet, yelling into his face. "You stupid punk! You came *that* close, *that* close! We were about to ventilate that thing to protect us all... And you would have been the collateral damage!"

Melvin's laughter quickly fell away as he realized that Burt was not joking, and he had almost got shot.

"One of these days, Melvin," Earl said, "somebody's gonna kick your ass six ways from Sunday."

Walter rushed over to rescue his precious creature. "Dammit! This isn't a toy! You mess it up, who's gonna pay? Not you, that's for sure. I should sue your parents for potential damages and lost revenue... Unbelievable!"

Not paying attention to any of it, Val and Earl stood gazing nervously out across the vast desert. The one that would soon be filled with incredible heat, and something murderous.

Burt walked over and clapped them on their shoulders. "Well... you fellas watch yourselves, you understand?"

Nancy called out from the store's doorway. "Come back with the Sheriff."

"Sheriff? Like hell, Nancy," Nestor said, finally saying something after watching everyone silently. "You better come back with the damn National Guard."

As Val and Earl got on the horses and urged them forward, a scatter of voices called out; "Keep your heads down," "Go careful, boys," "Keep a sharp lookout," a worried farewell that made both of them feel even warier about what they may have gotten themselves into.

The sun climbed in the sky the further Val and Earl rode.

They looked like specks of dirt against the endless sweep of desert around them, just two very on-edge men in a land suddenly too big, too empty and too dangerous.

"What if Miguel is right and the snake had nothing to do with it?" Val said. Clearly worried about jumping to conclusions too.

Earl didn't look worried at all. "Then there's a guy

out here killing people. Either way we got a way to stop 'em… Besides, when we get to Bixby, we send the cops back, maybe we stay there, secure the jobs and come back for our stuff later?"

"Sounds like a plan," Val smiled, letting the worry disappear.

Earl moved back and forth in his very uncomfortable saddle, looking at the horizon uneasily. "But you know what," he said, quietly, "ain't no way we can make Bixby by nightfall, is there? Not on these mules."

Val groaned in frustration. He didn't want to hear that, even if it was true. He just wanted to get out, but each step the horses took felt further away from safety.

Earl continued, "and that means we're gonna be out here... like, in the dark."

"Great. Thank you very much, Perfection," Val scowled. "Thank you for sending us all the way out here, 'cause you're all too chicken shit to do it yourselves. We ain't even staying, why the hell did we say okay?"

Earl shook his head in agreement. They did not choose this, but how could they say no? Who else would it have been? Burt and Heather had to stay to protect everyone... So Walter? Melvin? They both may have hated that they were nominated to go, but they knew they were the best choice.

Ahead, faint strains of music drifted on the humid breeze.

They were finally nearing Jim and Megan Wallace's house.

Aside from the muted music, Jim and Megan's place was eerily quiet as Val and Earl rode up.

"You hear that?" Earl asked.

The trailer door was wide open, flapping against the wall, as Val got off his horse, and walked over. He rapped upon it, knocking harder than necessary, expecting to hear a reply from inside.

"Doc...?" he said loudly.

But no one replied.

Leaning in, he looked around the trailer.

"Empty," he mumbled.

Turning, he saw Earl emerging from the half-finished house, shrugging.

"They must've made it to Bixby," he said, as he then realized what could be heard. "You *do* hear that, don't ya?" Earl added, looking around. "Is it comin' from the trailer?"

"Nope." Val shivered as he shook his head. "Oh, man, I hate this shit."

"We need the guns," Earl said.

Val didn't need to reply as they both walked briskly back to their horses. Earl yanked Heather's heavy rifle from the saddle scabbard, as Val grabbed his battered Winchester.

Walking around the property, with guns ahead of them, neither of them felt brave.

"So, the car's not here," Earl stated, trying his best to sound confident over his nerves. "We just missed 'em, that's all… So, we should just head on to Bixby. Ride all night. To hell with sleep."

Val wasn't buying it, something was off. "If they're gone, then where's the goddamn song coming from?"

The music wasn't drifting from the house or the trailer.

Val moved cautiously in the direction of the sound, rifle raised, eyes looking in every direction. Earl followed, preferring his option of just going, but raising his rifle too.

Getting to where the car had disappeared, both could see that the ground had been torn, churned and disturbed. And as they got closer, they both realized that the music was coming from… down.

"It's like Fred's sheep pen… But without the blood," Earl thought out loud. "What happened here?"

Val scuffed at the dirt with his boot.

A flash of glass immediately caught the sun, as a weak beam of light glowed.

Val dropped to his knees, sweeping at the dirt, revealing the headlight from Jim and Megan's station wagon, as well as the vehicle's crumpled grille. But not just that. As he wiped the sand and dirt away, something sticky and red smeared on his palms. Blood that stained the dirt around the car.

Earl gulped. "Or maybe it's *exactly* like the sheep pen."

Val frantically rubbed his hand on his jeans and he

stood up, looking sickened. "It's blood!" he gasped. "It's frickin' *blood*!"

Within seconds, they were riding at full gallop across the open desert, pushing the chubby, old (and now also terrified) horses to their limits. They soon got to a barbed-wire fence and followed it along a concrete-lined flood-control ditch.

"Goddamn it, Earl," Val shouted out. "What the hell did that? How could those snakes bury an entire Plymouth? Miguel was right, no way they could do that kind of shit!"

"I'm less concerned with how, and more concerned with why," Earl countered, shouting back over the wind. "*Why* would anyone or anything do it? For what possible—"

In unison, the horses ground to a stop, cutting off Earl's words. They neighed and balked, in a sudden frenzy. They started to rear up and refused to go any further.

Fighting the reins, Earl and Val struggled to control the horses as they whirled and sidestepped.

"I knew it!" Val shouted. "Walter wouldn't know a decent horse if—"

"Shut up!" Earl barked back, quickly drawing his rifle. "They got wind of something they don't like!"

"Aw shit!" Val also whipped the Winchester from his shoulder.

With the horses still acting up, they both spun in

their saddles, scanning the barren desert through their sights.

But nothing moved out there except them.

"I don't see anything!" Val said, his heart now hammering loudly in his ears.

Then, by total surprise, Earl's horse went down with a pained bray. It crumpled to the dirt, pitching Earl headfirst out of the saddle.

Val leaped off his horse and ran over to Earl, who groaned, winded but unhurt.

"Hey, you okay?" Val asked.

Earl didn't answer.

"*Earl*, you okay?" he repeated.

"Yeah... yeah..." Earl coughed, rolling onto his knees. "What about my horse?"

They both turned to where the horse fell, and stared, horror-struck.

Two thick snake-like things had latched onto the animal, dragging it down, crushing and slurping it into the earth. Taking the saddlebag of supplies and rifle along with it. With the creature around its throat, the thing stopped any neigh of agony coming from the horse's gasping mouth.

Val's horse meanwhile took the cue. It immediately bolted, galloping madly away from them across the flats.

"What in God's name is that?" Earl mumbled in wide-eyed horror.

"*That's* how they get you," Val almost screamed, dragging Earl backward. "They're a pack!"

Immediately they both realized the same thing. That the monster, the thing that had killed Fred. That had swallowed Jim and Megan's station wagon. The thing that now pulled the horse…

"They're under the goddamn ground!" Val shouted.

As the things dragged the strangled horse deeper down, they exchanged a silent look of fear.

Getting to their feet, they moved as fast as they could. Half running, half falling. They expected the things to lash out after them, but fifty yards on, a glance over their shoulders made both men slow to a stop. The things hadn't moved, and were still dragging the horse slowly under.

"What *are* they?" Earl said, staring at his horse's last moments. "They ain't no darn snakes!"

"They're sons of bitches, that's what!" Val grimaced, raising his Winchester. He sighted down the barrel and quickly fired.

The bullet hit its target, slamming into one of the things.

A spray of orange goo arced into the air, and a shriek echoed up through the sand, not from the creature, but from something below. As the things recoiled instantly, snapping back underground, they left the horse's front legs sticking out.

Both men heard the shriek and turned their eyes to the ground. As they watched, the dirt under their boots trembled, as it began to rise up. They stumbled and fell off the rising mount.

"There must be a million of them!" Val said.

The mound continued to surge upward, and soon split wide open.

From the depths, a massive head burst through the sand, covered in dirt and slime.

Looking like a mutation between a slug and a monster from a nightmare, its eyeless face ended in three tough, bony plates that closed together into a sharp point. As it rose, the plates cracked apart like a meaty flower, revealing a huge, oozing mouth. And inside that grotesque maw, the same snake-like things that had attached themselves to their truck's axle flailed. Its tentacles.

The creature's version of tongues and eyes. Its sharp and brutal tentacles.

Earl drew the pistol from his belt, his hand trembling as it gripped. "Nope, not millions of 'em," he said hoarsely. "Just… one… big… bastard."

They then opened fire, shooting their weapons with zero restraint. The bullets hit their targets, but barely affected the monster, as the slugs crumpled and fell to the ground from their armored hide.

The large slug-like thing then swung its huge head toward them, and its bony plated mouth opened wide, as it belched out a hideously furious roar, then snorted and snuffed, sounding like an angry boar.

Earl looked at his gun nervously.

"I don't think it worked," he said. "I think we just pissed it off."

As they both went to fire again, both the pistol and the rifle had run out of bullets.

"You got any ammo?" Val asked meekly, knowing the answer already.

The creature then lunged forward. Diving underground deep under the dirt and plowing forward like a whale through water.

The ground heaved as it tunneled right at them.

"This way," Val shouted in a panic as they ran sideways, sprinting along the barbed wire fence, dropping their useless weapons to the dirt.

The monster in chase, slammed into a fencepost from below, knocking the wood out of the ground. The barbed wire sagged on impact.

As they kept running for their lives, the thing hit fencepost after fencepost. Each one was launched flying into the air by the goliath burrowing beneath.

Val risked a glance back and immediately wished that he hadn't.

"It's gaining on us!" he cried out.

And as if that wasn't enough, Earl pointed desperately ahead of them.

To the flood-control ditch, which veered off in front of them. A wide concrete chasm, fourteen feet across, dead ahead.

They had no choice. Either they jumped and tried to clear the gap, or they fell into it.

"*We can do it*," Earl shouted. "*We can jump it!*"

They got to the edge at full sprint, and together they leaped…

. . .

Earl Bassett and Valentine McKee were no athletes. They were not even in shape. They both smoked and drank far too much for their bodies to do things that required peak physical condition.

Of course, they didn't make the ditch jump.

The creature churned through the earth behind, as they summoned every ounce of strength and jumped from the edge. Hurtling through the air…

…but only got as far as to slam onto the opposite side of the ditch, narrowly missing the top. They hit the concrete hard and tumbled back down the sloped wall to the ditch floor.

A beat later the creature hit the ditch. And hit it *hard.* It did not know that this concrete chasm lay in its path.

As it collided with the concrete like a locomotive at full speed, it smashed into the thick slab and cracked the stone outward, breaking it apart. From inside, one of the creature's tentacles flopped through the gap, twitching violently.

Val and Earl flinched, and got back up on their feet.

After a moment, the tentacle sagged limply and hung down the wall. Orange blood seeping from it, dripping down the pale stone embankment.

"What the…?" Earl said, panting hard more from

the shock than the exertion. "I guess Miguel was wrong."

Val crept closer to the beast poking out through the damaged wall. With his finger, he prodded the limp thing with a sharp poke. It did nothing.

"What a stupid son of a bitch," Earl said, trying to fathom what just happened. "It knocked itself cold."

Val prodded it again, and more orange ooze poured from the gashes all over it. A *lot* of ooze. "Out cold? My ass," he said. "This bastard's stone-cold dead."

A grin soon spread across his face. He raised his fist at the wrecked beast.

"You fucker!" he screamed triumphantly. His voice echoed off the canyon walls.

A moment later, they started to laugh. A giddy, nervous laughter, until a sudden rattle of pebbles behind them made them stop.

Standing on the far side of the ditch was Rhonda, lugging an armload of seismograph equipment, as well as a folding shovel tucked under her arm. She stared down at them, surprised and suddenly afraid at having weapons pointed at her.

"Hi, guys, what's going on?" she said nervously.

Relieved, they smiled.

"Sorry," Val said.

"It's okay… I… Can I ask…" Her nerves were still evident. "D-did you notice anything weird a minute ago? Vibrations or… or something? I mean, it just happened again… The-the readings…"

Val and Earl exchanged a look, then laughed helplessly all over again.

Rhonda's gaze moved to the cracked wall... and to the dead monster hanging out of it.

Her nervousness faded.

"What the hell is that?" she asked.

Later, as the desert sun continued to blaze overhead, Earl and Rhonda worked by the cracked ditch wall.

"Okay... let's go together," Earl said.

He and Rhonda were holding onto a fencepost they'd wedged into one of the broken parts of the concrete.

"One... two... Now!"

At once, they leaned all their weight onto the post, pushing down as hard as they could. Slowly, a large broken piece of concrete from the wall shifted. Peeling away with a grind as it fell out and thudded to their feet.

Through the broken chunks of wall, they had managed to remove, the creature's head was now fully exposed.

It was a horrifying sight: gushing orange blood, as the gaping, plated mouth hung slack and drooled a muddy, gravelly slime from within. Its tentacles lolled out like limp, glistening tongues.

"Jesus Christ," Earl said, eyes starting to water at the stench that came out of it.

Rhonda pinched her nose. "I don't see any eyes on

it… must be totally subterranean." She leaned a little closer, fascinated. "And those… tentacles, I guess?"

"I saw them shoot right outta its mouth," Earl said. "They hooked onto my horse and pulled it right down. Tried with our truck too." He shook his head as he spoke. "Good thing we stopped it before it killed anybody else. We think it already got a few people, and a load of sheep."

Rhonda shuddered. "Yeah. I'm lucky it didn't find *me*… I was just nearby." She wiped her brow with her sleeve, overwhelmed by the reality of it all. "This is all important, you know. This is like… well, let's just say, it's probably the biggest zoological discovery of the century." She gave a short, almost hysterical laugh. "The century? Forget that! Of history… Look at this thing." Her smile dropped, as she turned to him. "Wait… people are *dead?*"

Above them, a metallic *clang* echoed.

"I got it!" Val's voice called down. "Here's the other end! Just look at what we got here!"

Using the cracked rocks as a ladder, Rhonda and Earl climbed up the slope, ensuring not to step near the creature's goo.

Pulling themselves out of the ditch, they soon stood at the top and stared in astonishment at what Val had dug up.

The creature's entire massive body was now stretched before them, a thirty-foot leviathan partially unearthed in the desert floor. Val, using Rhonda's folding shovel, had just scraped away the last of the sandy dirt to reveal its thick, muscular tail.

It looked almost prehistoric… or perhaps alien.

"That is one big mother," Earl whispered.

Val smiled at Rhonda. "So, this is the guy that had your seismos on the blink?"

"I guess so, yeah," she nodded. She was unable to stop staring at the creature, as she moved closer, examining it.

The body was cigar-shaped, about five feet thick at the widest, and covered in dozens of short, rear-pointing retractable spikes. Rhonda poked at one gently with her foot. Instantly it sank inward like a plunger, and the neighboring spikes did the same, rippling in unison. A wave of movement across the skin.

Earl looked suddenly worried as he stepped. "I thought you said it was dead?" He gripped the empty gun in its holster.

"It *is*," Val assured.

"Well, those things over it just moved!"

"It's just a reaction," Rhonda explained. "You know, like a reflex."

Earl nodded, but he did not know. Not at all.

Rhonda continued her analysis. "It must push itself along with those things." As she spoke, she did so with wonder. "All of those little spikes, moving all at once. That's how it can go so fast. I mean, this thing was tripping sensors *all* over the valley. No wonder I couldn't…"

A chilling thought stopped her mid-sentence.

Without another thought, she ran back down into the ditch and picked up her backpack, pulling out a handful of her seismograph printouts.

Earl peered down at her from the ridge, puzzled. "Hey, you ever heard of anything like this before? Is this a thing usually in Nevada? Must play up sensors often, right?"

Val elbowed him. "Sure, Earl. *Everybody* knows about 'em. We just didn't tell you. It's a huge conspiracy."

Earl didn't look amused.

"Come on," Val said. "*Nobody's* ever seen one of these! We're really in on something here! This could make us a bunch of cash!"

"Walter *cannot* get his sticking mitts on this for no measly fifteen bucks!" Earl added, realizing the potential. "It's *our* find."

"You got that right," Val agreed.

They grinned, basking in a moment of mutually imagined fame.

"Here's a plan," Earl said. "We'll get a… flatbed. A real big one. I guess one with a huge winch on it. Figure a five ton."

"Nah, you don't wanna winch it," Val replied. "That'd tear it all up. We need to lift it all at once. With a crane and some lifting straps, like when they transport elephants."

Earl looked at Val in total confusion.

Meanwhile, back in the ditch, Rhonda's face had gone pale as she poured over her printouts.

"Hey, hey, shut up!" she said suddenly, over their loud plan, trying to figure out all the data.

Val looked to Earl, who shrugged.

They then both climbed down the ditch.

"What is it?" Earl asked.

"The way I figure it," she said, intently staring at the papers. "There's gotta be three more of these things out there."

"Three?" Earl asked quietly. "You gotta be shittin' me."

Rhonda jabbed at the inked lines on her charts, flipping from one page to the next as she stood up. "Yeah, look. I've got readings from all over the valley. If you compare the different data charts, there has to be three of them left. Here's one at two o'clock yesterday." She flipped another sheet. "But here's another one, three miles away, at the same time. That's two. And here—"

They didn't need to hear any more.

"We'll take your word for it," Val said urgently.

They walked over, grabbed her by the arms and hustled her back up the other side of the ditch.

"Where's your truck?" Earl asked as they got to the top.

"Other side of that dome!" Rhonda said, motioning behind her, to a rough, boulder-strewn hill rising out of the sandy desert soil like a cluster of giant mushrooms.

"But we gotta finish studying this," she complained.

"If there's three more," Earl replied. "We're going, now…"

"There could be one right under us right now," Val

added. But as he did, he slowly stared down, realizing that it was very, very possible.

Rhonda and Earl realized too.

As they broke into a sprint, they ran from the ditch in a blind panic, imagining the things would leap out of the ground at them at any moment.

Passing one of the seismograph stations, Earl's stride faltered as the ground beneath him crumbled inward. His foot had broken through the surface, and his leg plunged into a hole that now opened up. He yelped as he fell into the hole, stopping waist deep.

Val was immediately behind him, with his hands under Earl's armpits, yanking him back out with all his strength.

As Earl got to his feet, all three looked around at each other panting. Taking a look at the hole, Earl rolled his eyes. Not a snake slug thing…"

"No?" Rhonda asked.

"It's a damn prairie dog burrow."

"Little sons of bitches," Val moaned.

Rhonda tensed, suddenly hearing a sound she knew all too well. The nearby soft scratching of a seismograph needle across the paper cylinder.

She whacked Val on the arm and pointed speechlessly at the station.

Even from where they were, they could see that the needle was going berserk.

They started to run again.

As they did, they could hear a rumbling building deep below their feet. Like a mobile tremor, what sent the needle into a frantic spin was now moving closer, and as it did the ground began to visibly shake along with it.

"On the rocks!" Rhona shouted, pointing to the largest of the boulders ahead. One where the remains of an old rail fence lay scattered at its base.

They scrambled over the wood and iron, crawling up the rockface.

"It can't get us up here, can it?" Earl asked Rhonda, as if she were the oracle of all.

"It's probably just gonna slam into the rock like before," Val said hopefully.

Rhonda stared silently at the sand below, that was shifting from the large mass underneath. One that suddenly slowed as it got nearer to the boulders.

Breaching the sand near the fallen fence, three six-foot lengths of slimy tentacles emerged, slithering and questing along the base, blindly searching for them, but unable to get any nearer.

One of the tentacles that flipped over the rock below was shorter, ending in a bloody, mangled stump.

"Hey, look," Val said to Earl. "Bet that's the one that grabbed our truck."

"Well," Earl replied, stepping further up the boulder, "at least that bastard can't climb." He turned to Rhonda. "Pardon my French."

"Probably can't move too easily on the surface," Rhonda said. "But you never know."

"God," Val muttered, gagging as the stench from the

monster travelled up the boulder to them. "The live ones smell worse than the dead ones."

Below, the tentacles had finished feeling around, unable to find them, so slowly retracted, sliding back under the earth. And as they disappeared, the ground settled down flat once more, leaving them in an uneasy silence.

"Okay," Earl said. "Now... How far's your truck?"

Rhonda pointed across the boulders.

They could see the vehicle's roof glinting faintly in the sun, maybe a hundred yards away.

Val looked at the open space they would need to cross to get there. "I don't know about that," he said. "If this one's any faster than the last one, we'd be eaten for sure."

"Good point," Earl nodded, having no ambition to run again for his life anytime soon. "I think we should wait *right* here... It's probably gonna give up soon."

The minutes turned to hours, dragging by them in the stifling heat.

Still sat on the sun-bleached boulder, the three of them had little to do but theorize what was now happening.

"I've never seen anything like them in the fossil records I've looked at around here, not that I've seen them all," Rhonda said, sitting cross-legged, her eyes half-closed in thought. "We gotta study that stuff in our first year... and you'd think if there was a record, I'd have been taught it… But these things could predate the fossil record…" She shook her head, discounting that thought. "No, that'd make them a couple of billion years old, and the likelihood we haven't ever seen one before now? The odds just don't stack up… Besides sand worms are mythological… Like unicorns."

"I vote for outer space," Earl chuckled, despite considering it as a valid option. "Came on a meteor or something." He stared at the cracked dirt around their rock perch. "No way those are local boys… They don't even look like any other animals I've ever seen."

"Well," Val added. "What about mutations caused by radiation? Atomic testing, like at Los Alamos? Or they could've been made in a lab. Government built them to be a *big* surprise for the Russkies."

Earl looked to the setting sun, then down to the motionless desert. "Well…it's been hours, and we haven't seen hide nor hair of them. Maybe it's long gone? Maybe needed to feed or drink someplace else?"

Val turned and shot him a skeptical look. "Or maybe it's right there. Why don't you take a little stroll and see?"

"Screw you too," Earl retorted, then turned to Rhonda. "Pardon my French."

Rhonda sighed. "Well, we've gotta do *something*. Can't just sit here forever."

They all sat in silence, agreeing but not having a clue what to do.

Val's eyes then lit up. He got to his feet and walked slowly down the boulder.

"What are you doing?" Earl called out after him.

With caution, Val edged down to the side of the boulder, and picked up a broken fence post, holding it up as a weapon.

"Watch yourself," Earl warned. "It's got a good six-foot reach."

Val nodded as he crouched low to the rock. Reaching out he held the post above the sand.

"Careful," Rhonda added.

Taking in a few short, sharp breaths, Val forced a confident smile, getting the nerve. "It's long gone," he whispered, lowering the post and tapping it lightly against the sand.

The reaction was instant.

The ground exploded beneath the post in a cloud of sand. Tentacles shot out, lashing, grabbing the wood tightly and ripping it with ease out of Val's grasp.

"Damnit!" Val shouted, nearly toppling forward as he quickly ran up the rock, back to safety. "Hot damn son of a bitch!" he gasped.

"Sons of *goddamned* bitches!" Earl repeated. "Been waiting there all this time! How the hell's it even know we're still here?"

Val shook his head, exasperated. "It's got no eyes, right? And it sure as hell can't smell anything underground, not over its own stink. So, it could have like superman hearin' and been down there all this time listenin' to us!"

Rhonda stared with realization. "Of *course!*" she said, snapping her fingers. "It senses seismic vibrations.

It hears every move we make, especially on this rock. It's a perfect conductor for all noise. You make a small step, it's amplified downward. Why didn't I think of that? It's literally what I do! It's all about sound."

Earl slumped back. "So, what you're sayin' is we're stuck."

Rhonda didn't want to answer, as that would make it all too real. She pulled her knees up closer to her chest. "When I was a kid, I always wanted to be stranded on a desert island, but somehow I always imagined, you know... water."

"And no stinking' slug monsters," Val added.

The sun dipped behind the hills, and the desert started to lose its heat, bringing a chill among them. Against the blackening sky, littered with a million stars, their silhouettes huddled together on the rock.

After at least an hour where no one had spoken, Earl looked more and more uncomfortable, until he had to say something.

"You know," he said, "I hate to be crude, but I'm gonna have to take care of some... business here, if you get what I mean."

"Me too," Val added immediately, having been holding his bladder for a while.

"Same here," Rhonda added without a trace of embarrassment.

"Each take a corner?" Earl suggested.

They then moved awkwardly in the dark to opposite

sides of the rock, disappearing into the shadows around them. In the silence, the soft sound of zippers carried, followed by the sound of dripping water.

There was a communal sigh of relief from the men.

Then, from the darkness:

"Darn it!" Rhonda's voice.

"You okay?" Val called out.

"Yeah," she answered, clearly irritated. "But I'll tell you, if you ever wanted proof that God's a man, this is it."

CHAPTER 5

PARDON MY FRENCH

The dawn followed the night, and the desert around lay still and lifeless. The sky rose and brightened the land into rich bands of orange and red.

On the boulder, Val was already awake, looking confused. He had woken with a start, sat bolt upright and now glanced around in confusion. His jacket was no longer draped over him as he had left it. He was freezing.

Turning, he soon noticed that Rhonda, who was waking too, had his jacket wrapped snugly around her shoulders.

As she woke, she blinked sleepily, then noticed Val's puzzled look at her. Realizing what was keeping her warm, she frowned slightly. She had no memory of how it got there. Hurriedly, she took the jacket off and handed it back, with a look of embarrassment at his presumed chivalry.

"Thanks," she said, sheepishly.

Val glanced sideways at Earl, who had suddenly become very interested in his boots, avoiding all eye contact. He said nothing about having woken in the night, seen her shivering, and moved Val's jacket onto her.

"No problem," Val said, taking the win and hiding his annoyance. "Anytime."

Earl fished through his pockets, pulling out the crumpled pack of cigarettes but no lighter. Val reached into his shirt pocket and came up with a lighter but no cigarettes. As they did every morning, they swapped and each lit up.

Earl exhaled on his second puff and said, "Well, folks, it's morning. A brand-new day. What's the plan of action?"

Val grabbed the piece of wood that he had next to him all night and threw it out into the sand.

They watched it sail through the air gracefully.

The second it hit the ground, the earth bulged and stirred. Something massive moved toward the spot with a low, whispering rustle. Tentacles broke through and pulled the wood down with it again.

"That's a no then," Earl said.

"Doesn't he have a home to go to?" Val said. "We damn well do… kinda."

The depressing reality was starting to settle in. "This is why Edgar never got down off that tower, ain't it?" he added.

Earl nodded, wishing to hell they had been wrong about everything.

Rhonda, staring around at the surrounding boulders, suddenly brightened. "I might have an idea… Not a great one… but it's an idea!"

Her words fell on deaf ears as Val and Earl were already in deep discussion.

"We're gonna have to come up with *something*," Earl said, frowning. "Or it's just gonna wait us to death. We can't stay here waitin' to dry up."

"Let's just run for it, then," Val said. "We outran one yesterday, right?"

Rhonda gave up any thought to interject as they were too busy standing in their own way. She got up and walked down to the edge of the boulder, grabbed a long metal crossrail from the broken fence, and balanced it carefully in her hands.

Earl shook his head, not seeing what she was doing, still talking to Val. "Running's not a plan. Running's what you do when the plan fails."

Val shrugged. "Not like we've got a hell of a lot of options."

"You guys know how to pole vault?" Rhonda called over to them.

They turned, confused, staring at her.

Without hesitation, she charged forward, cross rail held out straight, down the side of the boulder. Lowering the rail, she caught the end of it in the sand and vaulted cleanly over the fifteen-foot gap to the next rock.

A second later, the ground around the pole erupted. A tentacle burst upward, slashing at the empty air, but she was already safe atop the next rock, and had taken the metal pole with her.

Val and Earl exchanged stunned yet incredibly impressed glances.

"We just stay where it can't get us," Rhonda shouted over. "Move across the boulders like this. My truck's parked right next to one."

Val turned to Earl and spoke quietly. "She doesn't know that they can pull trucks down does she?"

"Better this than running across the sand though, right?" Earl replied as he stood up. Walking over to the boulder edge, he picked up two more cross rails. Shoving one into Val's hands.

"Stay on the boulders," he said with a confident grin. "Easy as apple pie."

Taking a quick breath, he nodded to Val before breaking into a run. Vaulting with all his strength.

The pole was held out.

It was then lowered.

Its end hit the sand on target.

He was lifting in the air, pulled up from the boulder by the pole.

But that was as far as he went.

He had gotten about six feet off the ground, then flopped back onto the rock, and onto his ass.

He was embarrassed but alive. He pulled the pole back out of the sand, before the tentacles soon burst up looking for it.

Val grinned and moved into position. It was his turn.

"Come on, old man," Val said. "Just look out for your hip."

After a few more attempts, Earl had gotten the hang of it, and soon all three were crossing the boulders with ease. Vaulting from one to the other, getting more confident with each leap. It was a strange sight: two handymen and a geologist pole vaulting in the scorching heat.

Finally, they each landed on the nearest boulder to Rhonda's truck, which was still a good ten yards away over open sand.

Earl didn't look convinced. "That slimebag ain't gonna give us much time once we hit that truck, and even then, it could grab the wheels and…" his words trailed off. "I say the best choice we got is if we all jump together to cut down how much time he'll have."

Val and Rhonda nodded, but not liking the plan. It was, though, their only option. Safety in numbers.

Rhonda stuck the truck keys between her teeth.

"We all ready?" Val asked.

"As I'll ever be," Earl replied, not wanting to go.

"On three?" Val said.

On the third count, they vaulted in unison. Across the sand and landed with a hard crash in the bed of the pickup, aside from Val, who misjudged and went too far, heading to the sand on the other side. Earl quickly reached up and grabbed him back down to the truck.

With a shaken look on his face, having come close to becoming an open target, Val nodded to Earl in thanks.

Rhonda immediately jumped to the cab, squeezing headfirst through the rear sliding window.

"Come on," Earl urged quietly. "Go, go, go—"

The truck jolted violently upward, as something underneath slammed into it. The vehicle soon came crashing back down. Dust and rocks flying all around them.

Half-hanging through the window, Rhonda flailed inside, slapping blindly at the ignition. With the key finally making its way in, the engine howled to life. She pushed herself in further, legs still hanging out of the window, and had no option but to floor the gas with her hand. The truck ran forward, tires spitting sand behind it.

Before they could get away, a tentacle lashed upward and tore the truck's muffler clean off the engine, as other tentacles shot upward, reaching over the side for them.

Both Val and Earl grabbed some of the geological equipment from around them, and began to swat the tentacles away, like it was baseball.

"GO! GO! GO!" Val bellowed, smashing one spiked tentacle aside with a hand trowel.

The truck moved very fast, and for a second both men felt a wave of relief...

…Only to realize Rhonda was driving upside down, legs hanging out the back window, with her hand jammed on the gas pedal, not able to see where she was going.

On the edge of town, Mindy Sterngood bounced happily on her pogo stick beside one of the old, abandoned shacks. She looked up as a battered, mufflerless truck came into view, loud and trailing of gray smoke that billowed from the engine behind it. Rhonda, now sitting behind the wheel, was barely managing to keep the vehicle under control as she raced as fast as she could toward the store.

When it got outside, before the wheels even had a chance to stop spinning, Val was jumping from the back and sprinting for his own pickup.

"I'm gonna round everybody up," he called over his shoulder. "Meet you back here!" As he ran, he looked back at Earl and held his hand up high.

Earl nodded, took the truck key from his pocket and tossed it over without hesitation. Val caught it with a smile, got in the truck and was gone before Rhonda even had a chance to turn her own engine off.

She got out and walked around the back of her truck, assessing the damage to the rear undercarriage. She shook her head in annoyance. "Aw, shit," she mumbled. "That was a brand-new muffler as well. I'm sure the insurance company doesn't cover acts by sand worm."

"I'll bet you're sorry the college ever sent you up here," Earl said.

Rhonda stood, tossing her tangled hair out of her face. "Well, I'm scared, I'll admit that," she said. "But I'm not sorry at all. This is exciting. It's a new discovery! And for geology, biology, history, it could answer lots of questions!"

Earl looked at her curiously.

"You know what," he said casually, "Val went to your college too?"

"Really? The Val that just drove away?"

"Yeah, for a whole year. Couldn't quite sit still for it, though. Had too much vinegar in his system. You got a lot in common."

Rhonda raised an eyebrow, already seeing where this was going.

"But once he settles down, forgets that damn cowboy stuff..." Earl shrugged. "He'll be one in a million, you'll see that."

She smiled politely, catching the full awkward clumsiness of his pitch.

Earl grinned, knowing how obvious he was being. "All right, I'm about as subtle as a donkey's ass. Pardon my French. I'm just saying, the boy's got potential, that's all."

As they reached the store, Rhonda found herself wondering about his friend too.

· · ·

An hour later, Nestor, Melvin, Nancy, and Miguel all clustered around Val, Earl, and Rhonda. Walter sat off to one side behind the counter, fiddling with a CB radio, trying and failing to raise Burt and Heather.

"No, no," Val said, busily explaining, shaking his head. "The snake things are just their tongues, or something. These animals are frickin' huge. Like monster truck size slugs with big mouths."

Everyone stared, struggling to process the whole prospect.

"So… not snakes?" Miguel asked. "And we know for sure that these big things are the ones that did all this? To Fred? To Edgar? Jim and Megan?"

"I'm sorry," Nancy said, one eyebrow raised. "I'm having a real difficult time with this."

"Hey, Walter," Earl cut in, looking around the room, "any luck?"

Walter frowned as he hung up the CB with a frustrated moan. "Can't raise 'em," he said. "I guess they're still out there somewhere."

Rhonda looked up at Miguel and offered a comforting smile. "I think these things did take your friends."

Miguel nodded. Not liking it but having to accept it. "Hey, what are they called?"

Nestor perked up immediately. "Yeah, and where'd they come from?"

"I don't know." Rhonda replied.

"But you're a scientist, right?" Walter pressed.

"You oughta have a theory or something," Melvin added.

Rhonda threw her hands up. "Look, these creatures are absolutely unprecedented! No one knows about them. No one has named them."

Nestor wasn't giving up. "Yeah, but where'd they *come* from?"

Exasperated, Rhonda snapped, "Where'd they come from? Okay, worms. Probably in the Jurassic period. Cosmic radiation was much higher back then, so they mutated, and they got so big they just sank right into the ground and fell asleep. Hibernated... And now continental drift has brought them back to the surface, ready to be harvested by ancient alien meat-growers who planted them here."

Everyone stared at her, deadpan.

Then the tension broke, a few nervous smiles spreading.

Earl chuckled. "Hey guys, it don't matter where they come from, only that they are here, and we gotta fight."

Walter leaned over his counter eagerly. "No name, huh? Well, we discovered them. We should name 'em! That's how it's done, right? Finders namers."

"Oh, come on." Val moaned. "We should be talking about what we're gonna do. Earl and me think we better get out of here right now."

"You think we're not safe here?" Miguel asked, looking suddenly worried.

"Ask me after you meet one," Val replied. "I think

we all need to get the hell out while the going's good, and don't be on the sand at all."

"Hang on, Val," Nestor said, sounding quite annoyed. "Let's not go off half-cocked and just run."

"Exactly," Nancy nodded. "Someone's bound to come and check on us. I mean, once they see the road's out, and the phone lines are down... There are people who'll come for us. Government. Army. Whatever."

"Yeah," Nestor agreed. "That's exactly how this stuff works. The government has systems in place. Processes."

Miles away, beyond the rockslide on the canyon road, the truth was a bloody mess.

The road workers' utility truck still sat abandoned near the landslide. But not far from it, on the other side of the rock pile, a telephone maintenance vehicle truck had pulled up. Its emergency lights flashed silently in the heat. Scattered nearby, two hard hats lay cracked in the dust. Around them lay fragments of climbing gear, tool belts, and a still smoldering cigar. All had been covered in a whole heap of blood spatter.

In Walter's, the debate raged on.

Melvin and Walter were brainstorming monster names, apparently oblivious to the mounting fear.

"How about Mega Worms?" Melvin suggested.

Walter stuck his finger in the air, feeling a Eureka

moment. "Suckers. Suckoids." He paused, thinking. "I like 'oid'… What about Snakeoid?"

Meanwhile, Val, Earl, and Rhonda were gathering the serious-minded ones, Nancy, Nestor and Miguel, around the faded map on the wall.

"One of 'em comes near me," Nestor said, puffing up, "I'll just nail it with a five-pound pickaxe."

Earl shook his head. "Nestor, you're not getting it. It's the size of a damn airstream… They come up under you. Grab you before you even know what hit you. No pickaxe'll do a damn thing."

"They can sense the slightest vibration through the ground," Rhonda added. "Even footsteps. That's how they hunt. And they're bound to find us here, sooner or later."

Miguel clutched the brim of his hat. "So… like if we don't vibrate, right? Maybe they won't even come. Maybe they'll leave us alone. I can stay still."

Val stabbed his finger at the map. "They *are* headed right for us," he said. "Look. They trapped Edgar here. They grabbed Old Fred here. Ate his sheep and asshole dog. Nailed those poor suckers on the road. The doc's place, then where I got one with Rhonda."

He didn't need to explain. They got it. The dots formed a line, a straight, inevitable line, leading straight to Perfection.

"This valley's just one long smorgasbord," Val said. "And we've got to get out. If we don't haul ass soon, we're gonna be the next course."

They stared at him in silence.

Nancy suddenly looked worried. "Oh no… Mindy?"

She hurried out, Melvin trailing after her.

Walter, undeterred, clapped his hands. "What about Graboids? Huh? *Graboids*!"

Earl groaned. "Jesus, Walter…"

"We're gonna be sorry if they don't have a name," Walter insisted, "and Graboids…. That sounds timeless!"

Nestor looked at Val. "Okay, so you're saying we gotta get out. If they are as dangerous as you say they are, then where're we supposed to go? You keep saying we have to go, but where to?"

Val motioned to Rhonda. "She's got an idea about that."

All eyes turned to her.

She took a breath. "See, they move easily through the Pleistocene alluvials," she said.

Her words only earned her blank looks.

"Sorry," she said, rolling her eyes. "I'm in college mode… The *dirt*. Loose soil that makes up the valley floor. It's called Pleistocene alluvials… So, they move fine through that, but they can't move through solid rock. We saw that firsthand. So, we should go where there is rock."

"You know," Earl said, nodding, "up the jeep trail."

"Right," Rhonda nodded. "Those mountains are solid granite. We'd be safe there. We could hike along them… all the way to Bixby, if we have to. Wouldn't have to touch any loose dirt once."

A sudden movement.

Something had shot through a nearby open window and smacked Earl squarely in the chest. He flailed backward, cursing, until he realized what it was.

A basketball.

Outside, Melvin was doubled over with laughter.

Furious, Earl picked up the ball and hurled it back at him. A shot the kid easily dodged.

"You little asswipe!" Earl shouted out. "You knock that off or you'll have to shit out that basketball after I shove it down your damn throat!" he turned back to see Rhonda staring at him shocked. "Pardon my French!" he quickly added.

"Mindy?" Nancy called out as she reached the abandoned shacks. She slowed, looking around nervously.

"Mindy? Baby?" she called again, her voice trembling.

There was no answer.

Back at Walter's, Melvin was up to his usual antics, circling around the back of the store, bouncing his basketball in a steady rhythm onto anything he could. Inside, the voices of the townsfolk carried out to him.

"Well, you all do what you want," Nestor said, as stubborn and defiant as he always was. "No way I'm leaving my home."

Val's reply was sharper. "It's gonna take us *days* to get back with help. What you gonna do 'til then? Sit around with your thumb up your ass?"

"Damn it, Nestor, we're not going to leave you here to die," Earl added.

Melvin tutted as he tuned them out, focusing instead on the satisfying *thump, thump, thump* of the ball against the dirt… until, abruptly, the calming rhythm stopped.

His basketball hit the ground with a soft *flup* and didn't come back up.

He stared down for a few seconds. Confused.

The ball was gone. Only a swirl of dust marked the spot where it had vanished.

Inside the store, everyone jolted at the sudden scream from outside. Obviously, it was Melvin, but the sound was sharper and more terrified than any he had made before.

"I'm gonna kick his dumb ass across the damn state," Earl growled, storming to the door. "Pardon my French," he added.

"And I'm gonna help you with that," Val agreed, striding behind him.

They marched out of the store and around the building, boiling with fury, only to find nothing. Just the hot sand, the empty street, and the low whine of wind stirring around.

Then they heard it, a soft, shuddering whimper, coming from above.

They looked up.

There was Melvin, clinging halfway up a telephone pole like a cat chased up a tree, his face full of terror. His pants leg was shredded, his calf bloodied.

This was no prank.

Val and Earl stopped moving, suddenly feeling the vibrations of something moving below them. Moving up toward them.

Without a word, they leapt away from each other, just as the earth erupted where they had stood. A massive, gaping mouth lunged out, tentacles thrashing wildly, missing them by mere inches.

Screams came from every direction, as the rest of the townsfolk had come outside and now saw what had broken up through the ground.

They almost tripped over each other in a frantic stampede.

Nestor sprinted straight for his trailer. Melvin, somehow still hanging on to his senses, dropped from the pole and scampered to a nearby corrugated tin shed. The rest of them all hurried back into Walter's store, slamming the doors behind them.

"Jesus Christ!" Miguel gasped. "Whose got a gun?!"

"What are we gonna do?!" Walter cried, fumbling at the counter.

"Quiet!" Rhonda hissed. "QUIET!"

The command cut through the air like a straight razor.

Then, from outside, a faint snuffling sound could be heard, pig-like and wet.

Then there was silence again.

Everyone stopped.

All except Viola's gargoyle-looking dog, which had for the last hour been so quiet, everyone had forgotten it was there. But now, it was in full force, yapping incessantly as Viola held it tight.

"Shhh!" she said in a frantic whisper. "I'm done babysittin' ya!"

"Shut that thing up," Earl seethed.

"Don't it look like I'm tryin'?" Viola whispered back.

Around them, the sound came of a terrible groaning, as the entire building creaked and shifted on its foundations. And the more it did, the more the dog barked. Something was moving deep underneath, attracted by the sound.

"Please, please, please shut your cakehole!" Viola said as she tried to hold the dog's mouth shut, but the animal was too determined to make a god-awful racket.

The store rose up off its foundations, bottles clinked behind the bar. A faucet juddered. The floorboards creaked, and Viola lost her grip on the dog, who jumped from her hands and ran over to the other side of the store, barking at the floorboards.

Somewhere below, the creature moved, brushing against the pipes under the floor. The smell of the creature seeped up through the dirt. The smell of wet earth, death, and rot. A smell the dog loved.

"Get back here!" Viola pleaded, chasing after the dog, managing to grab hold of the leash trailing from its collar.

"Just let it go!" Earl said.

"Viola!" Val shouted.

But it was too late. The floor at the far end of the shop broke open right beneath the dog, and the tentacles burst up, dragging it down in an instant.

Viola was just as unlucky, as the leash was dragged down into the hole as well, and she had no time to think, so she still held onto it tightly.

Within a few seconds, both the dog and Viola were swallowed into the ground by the tentacles.

Everyone stood in shock. Earl was about to shout out, when Rhona put her hand out to cover his mouth, motioning for him to be quiet.

"Shhh," she said as softly as possible.

Each of them stood there, staring at the hole in the shop. Not knowing what to say or do. They were helpless to stop what happened.

Rhonda whispered pointedly. "No noise. No vibration."

They obeyed, standing still, barely daring to breathe.

From the distance, another sound came, innocent and familiar.

Thomp. Thomp. Thomp.

Val turned to the window; his stomach dropped.

Mindy, blissfully unaware, was bouncing along the

empty street on her pogo stick, her Walkman blaring in her ears. Her mother had not found her, and Mindy had heard nothing except her music.

The others looked horror-struck.

"*Mindy!*" Val suddenly shouted. "Get off your pogo stick!"

"Run, Mindy!" Earl yelled.

"Quiet!" Rhona hissed again.

They screamed over each other, but Mindy, lost in her music, did not hear a word.

She just pogoed along.

Thomp. Thomp. Thomp.

Around her as she got nearer to the store, the ground beneath her began to shudder. Getting stronger and stronger the nearer she came.

Something massive was tunneling in her direction, locked in on the beat of her pogo stick.

Thomp. Thomp. Thomp.

Val didn't hesitate.

He jumped straight out of the window, without a care for his own safety and sprinted flat-out across the road.

Nancy, emerging from behind an abandoned trailer at the far end of town, spotted her daughter, and Val sprinting over to her.

"*Mindy!*" she screamed.

Mindy, oblivious, bounced in slow circles. Humming to her music.

Thomp. Thomp. Thomp.

She turned the pogo stick lazily on the beat. Lost in

her own world. Slowly looking up she inhaled with as sharp shock as she saw Val hurtling toward her.

He tackled her to the ground before she could even understand what was going on. They rolled together in a heap, as Mindy yelped indignantly.

"Oww! Val, you're hurtin' me," she shouted, only to have Val clamp a hand over her mouth.

He stared at the pogo stick. It did not fall to the ground as it should when he pulled her down. It stayed standing upright. She soon saw this as well, and her complaints dropped. Just in time to see it impossibly getting sucked straight down into the earth like a piece of loose spaghetti.

Nancy ran over, scooping Mindy into her arms, pulling her away from Val, who now urgently motioned for them to stay low and quiet, and most importantly, to listen.

They all crouched in the dust, straining to hear whatever they could.

Unexpectedly, the pogo stick exploded back up through the earth between them, shooting skyward with a cloud of dirt.

Val ran to the store, where Earl and Rhonda stood waiting on the porch.

Nancy and Mindy ran the other way, up the street to their house.

Thinking fast, Val made a beeline for his pickup, clambering over the tailgate, past scattered tools and junk, and onto the cab's roof.

Earl saw the ground breaking as the creature had

followed him, but had no time to warn before the truck was slammed into from underneath.

WHAM! A tire blew.

WHAM! Another hit, another tire.

The truck lurched, but Val clung on, holding onto the roof edge, as his eyes searched frantically. He then saw Earl and Rhonda.

There they stood, halfway between him and Walter's, having crept over to try and help him.

"*Get back, for Christ's sake!*" he yelled.

They hesitated.

Earl spoke quietly, as if the monster could hear them. "We gotta get him off there, it'll suck that whole truck down." Then his gaze jerked to a sudden noise coming from behind them.

A clattering of metal that came from the trailer down the street. As the ground moved, an old refrigerator sat outside in a garden toppled over, smashing on the ground.

"Oh Jesus," Earl breathed. "Rhonda…. There's another one comin'."

A second Graboid was indeed now tunneling toward them. The ground above it cracked as it traveled close to the surface.

Earl turned and bolted for Walter's, but Rhonda faltered. Then she had no time to run as the Graboid tunneled in front of her at speed, cutting off her path to follow.

Instead, she sprinted to the nearest shelter: a rusted, weed-covered shack.

She almost made it too.

With a jolt, she went sprawling face-first into the dirt, yanked to a halt by her leg being pulled back.

Something had her.

It was not a tentacle, but a wrapping of old, rusted barbed wire fence, lying hidden in the undergrowth, broken and discarded. A vicious concertina wire now clutching at her. She struggled, trying to wrench her leg free, but it had her tangled tight. The barbs close to cutting in.

Barely having a moment to reach down to free herself. The ground suddenly raised upward, and three tentacles slithered from below, searching for her. She rolled frantically to one side as one slimy tendril's tip slapped onto the dirt where her head had just been.

The tentacles reared up, ready for an attack. She rolled the other way as all three came down at once, narrowly missing her. As she had rolled the other way, the barbed wire dug in deeper, and she did all she could not to scream and cry out in pain.

She had to act fast, so gingerly grabbed the barbed wire, hands shaking, and pulled at it. The barbs ripped through her pants, scraping her skin, making her bleed… but she still couldn't break free.

The creature then found one end of the barbed fence on the floor. Its tentacles curled around the wooden post attached to one end of the wire and tugged at it, testing it like a spider sensing a trapped fly.

Then it yanked the post down into the earth, and straight away the creature breached, pulling its gargantuan mouth out of the ground, swallowing the post and first few feet of barbed wire.

Rhonda could not hold in her scream as the fence, and her along with it, was then dragged closer to the gaping, hideous monster. Her boots kicked up dust, heels dug frantically for purchase, for any hold to stop her being eaten.

The tentacles yanked harder and harder at the wire, pulling and pulling, and she slid closer.

The barbs now ripped deep into her legs, tearing her skin.

In a dead panic, she thrashed against the pull, grabbing desperately at the brush as she was dragged inch by inch nearer to its snapping jaws. Another vicious tug wrenched her *even* closer, close enough to feel the blast of hot, fetid breath from the depths of its guts. A putrid exhalation.

The truck wrenched from side to side. As the Graboid tried to pull it down into the earth, Val heard Rhonda's screaming.

Frantically, he searched the truck for a weapon, for anything he could use. Then he saw it. The pickaxe. The one that they never seemed to use.

He had no idea if he was being dumb or brave.

As Rhonda screamed again, kicking at the tentacles that were now attacking her, Val came charging into view, pickaxe held high.

The beast took another big gulp of the fence, dragging her closer and the tentacles battered down.

With a fierce yell, he swung the pickaxe wide in front of the open mouth, embedding it in one of the squirming tentacles. As the point cut into the beast's soft flesh with ease, it unleashed a torrent of orange gloopy blood, spraying all over them.

The creature shrieked, rearing up violently as it let out an ear-splitting, otherworldly sound. The pierced tentacle recoiled.

Val fumbled at Rhonda's boots, yanking them off.

"Come on! Outta your pants now!" he barked.

Rhonda didn't question his command. She pulled at her belt. But before she could free herself, her eyes widened in horror.

"*Look out!*" she screamed.

Behind him, the creature was coming again. Its tentacle stumps reaching out once more to grip onto the fence that pulled at her.

Val spun, pickaxe in hand, and began swinging it at the beast. But this time, one of the tentacles shot out and knocked the saw from his grasp. It fell to the ground with a large thunk.

The creature then moved back, readying itself to lunge at them. Without its full tentacles, it had to come closer if it wanted to feed.

Still on the floor, Rhonda kicked to wriggle free of her snared jeans. Val rushed behind her and grabbed under her arms. Pulling her back as hard as he could.

Stumpy, gory tentacles lashed out, as the mouth came closer.

With a final desperate heave from Val, Rhonda came free, leaving her boots and pants behind her, the wires cutting into her legs. They fell backward together just as the monster's mouth came down onto her jeans and consumed them in seconds.

There was no time to spare. Another eruption from the earth hurled dirt and debris into the air. The second creature burst up behind them, hungry, relentless with a mouth full of flailing tentacles.

Val and Rhonda rolled sideways and came up running, rushing to Walter's store along an old wooden sidewalk.

The second Graboid didn't pause, the sound of their steps on the wood was a loud signal for where they were going, and the creature was locked onto that sound.

As they ran, the boards behind them soon rippled and were thrown up as the creature passed directly underneath them.

Earl opened the door to Walter's just as they came into view, the boards churning behind them. The creature underneath, only a few steps behind.

"Come on! Come on!" Earl shouted. "Don't look back! Just run! Run like your ass is on fire!"

As they dove through the open door, the rippling boards surged past behind them, and around the store.

The creature did not realize that they had left the walkway.

Earl quickly eased the door shut as quietly as he could, sealing them inside.

Val looked up, confused and smiling. "Run like your ass is on fire?"

Earl glanced at Rhonda with a smile. "Pardon my French," he said.

CHAPTER 6

THE WAR AT HOME

The tension in the store was thick, and the heat was so close it was enough to choke on. Everyone moved around in slow careful motions, whispering every word they had to speak. With every misstep, where a creak sounded from the floorboards beneath them, it felt like a tightening of a noose around their necks. Outside, the town was as hot as an oven with an unrelenting sun at its apex.

Val crouched by Rhonda, iodine bottle in one hand, cloth in another as he gently dabbed onto the slashes on her legs. She didn't wince.

"You even payin' attention?" Val whispered. "This oughta be hurtin' like all hell."

"It does," she nodded. She had no idea her poker face was so good; it was agony. She was just doing her best to hide it. "So, is this one of your usual jobs as a handyman? Saving people's lives?"

Val smiled, slightly embarrassed. "First time for me, but I think I'm not too bad at it."

By the shelves, Earl watched them with a broad, Cheshire Cat grin.

Val caught his look, scowled back, and shook his head as if to say, *Knock it off.*

And Rhonda, catching the whole exchange, could not help but go red from embarrassment.

Walter soon crept out from the storeroom with a new pair of jeans, holding them aloft to Rhonda with a wink. Remembering their need for silence, he carefully handed the jeans over the counter to Earl, who passed them to Miguel, who passed them to Val, who passed them to Rhonda.

"Thank you," she mouthed gratefully.

"So, what are we gonna do?" Miguel said, barely audible, almost afraid to break the stillness with each syllable. "How long 'til they go away?"

"They got the patience of Job," Earl replied. "They just sit and wait 'til they hear something that sounds like lunch… We were on that rock all night, and it was still there the next mornin'… We need to make a plan."

With her wounds tended to, Rhonda slid on the new jeans. They were slightly too big but better than not wearing any at all. They painfully grazed each puncture wound as they were put on, but she hid it all.

Walter had an idea. "Hey, how about you and Val take your truck, get to the mountains, hike to Bixby, get us some help?"

Val shook his head. "Walter, those scumsuckers ate my radials. Truck's a lemon 'til we get new tires."

"My truck," Rhonda offered. "We can take mine then. Just missing the muffler. Still works though."

Earl shook his head again. "No good. You need serious four-wheel drive just to get up that trail. Yours would tap out halfway up, besides it's so loud now, they would be after us straight away."

Not paying attention, both Walter and Miguel reached for the same soda bottle on the counter. Their hands collided and the bottle was knocked off the counter.

Time slowed to a crawl as they all gasped, as the bottle seemed to take an age to land. Spinning through the air, falling to its inevitable conclusion.

"Damn," Earl said.

Crash.

The bottle smashed. Everyone held their breath and closed their eyes, waiting for impact.

Sure enough, the whole building suddenly shuddered. Floorboards creaked and bent as the ground moved underneath, and the *thwack*ing of tentacles searching and scraping the underside of the store could be heard.

After a few minutes, the noise subsided, and everyone relaxed, as much as they could.

"Well," Val whispered. "We're sure as hell not gonna survive here much longer if we can't even keep the noise down. We all gotta go."

Walter wasn't so sure. "Now wait a minute. I got

enough food here to last for weeks. Those damn things can't wait around forever. We can do it. If we have to. We *can* be quiet. I believe in us."

The words had barely left his mouth when the big freezer compressor switched on with a loud roar.

"Jesus!" Earl cried out. "Shut it off!".

Walter darted over to the freezer, but the power switch was buried behind towers of soft drink cases. He pulled at the stack, knocking them over in desperation. The crates toppled then crashed to the floor. Val and Earl quickly went to join him, needing it to be done a lot quieter.

But they were too late.

The floor splintered outward. A massive fleshy snout burst through, slamming Walter against the freezer. Its mouth opened and the tentacles lashed out. The barbs on their tips got hold of him, ripping into his flesh, getting a firm hold and dragging him back to the hole. One of the tentacles did not have hold. It flailed wildly, half of it missing. This was the same monster that had grabbed the truck's axle.

Earl, Val, and Miguel lunged to save Walter, grabbing any part of him they could as he screamed in pain. Earl held one arm. Val the other. Miguel grabbed his collar, but the monster's strength was beyond overwhelming. It jerked left and right, shaking Walter around like a doll, spinning him until the three were thrown aside.

As the creature sank back into the earth, pulling Walter down with it, one of his legs caught on the edge of the cracked floorboard, bending hideously backward, against the way it should. The tentacles got a firmer grip and yanked at him harder. Walter's screams tore through the store as his bones snapped, ribs cracked, flesh gouged open. Everyone tried to reach him. Tried to help him. But they were utterly helpless as he snapped clean in half, and the creature sank with its new meal under the store.

The last thing anyone saw of Walter Chang was his foot, folded up past his bloodied head.

Then, the rumbling faded away as the monster went to feast on his new Chinese meal.

Val stood shaking; fists clenched at his sides.

"Son of a bitch," he seethed in a tiny whisper. "Son of a *goddamn, ass sucking bitch.*"

Before they could regroup, another Graboid smashed up behind the counter. Then a third came up through the floor from under the tables, knocking them off their feet.

The store was now in a state of unbridled chaos as the two huge things roared and thrashed wildly. Tentacles whipped through the aisles, smashing items off the shelves, scattering flour, sugar, canned goods into the air.

Val quickly spotted the ceiling hatch.

"Everybody! This way! The roof! The roof!"

Rhonda, Miguel, Earl and Val raced through the wreckage to get there.

Val and Miguel slid sideways along the shelves, climbing frantically for the hatch.

Earl climbed a shelf and leapt from one to the other, grabbing Rhonda's hand as she fought to follow. But as she balanced precariously on the first shelf, one of the monsters came up behind her and rammed at her feet.

Jumping out of the way, she almost lost her balance as the shelf then tipped over.

The shelves then fell like dominoes.

One into the other they toppled.

Rhonda leapt, throwing herself after Earl, as he outran the cavalcade of shelving now following him. But she did not have time to catch up. She only had one option.

She turned and threw herself through one of the open windows, landing on the ground outside.

As Val saw her disappear, he turned and smashed at the ceiling hatch with a burst of newfound adrenaline, forcing it open and hauling himself on top of the store.

Miguel and Earl were on the roof, as Val leaned over the side and searched frantically for Rhonda.

"Where is she?" he said desperately to himself, before shouting out. "Rhonda? *Rhonda?*"

He soon heard a sharp whistle coming from behind him. Turning around, the three of them noticed that Rhonda had made it to the town's water tower just across the street. She was now scrambling up the rickety wooden ladder as fast as she could climb.

Below her, the ground rippled and shifted, as the

monsters heard her frantic steps, and were not too far behind.

Val yelled, "Keep moving! Don't stop! Don't look down!"

Rhonda, on the ladder, now higher than the buildings, naturally did what anyone would do when told to not look down: she looked down.

The ground below was mixing, lifting and sinking around the concrete anchors that the water tower's frame were built into. The monsters circled them closely, sizing them up.

Panicked, she climbed faster to the galvanized tank at the top. It was almost blinding to look at as the sun flashed off its corrugated metal body.

Terrified, Melvin peered out from the battered doorway of the storage shed he had hidden in, glancing up at the men now on top of the store's roof. With the water tower out of his view, he could not see any monsters or feel any of the ground trembling from where he was.

"Hey!" he called out. "What's going on?! What the hell you doing up there?!" His voice was high and shaky.

Miguel leaned out just enough to shout back, "Melvin, shut the hell up! What ya trying to do, get yourself killed?"

Melvin wanted to tell Burt to shut up in return, but right then, a violent *wham* shook the little shed he was in, sending a puff of dust up from the floor and filling the small space all around him, making him cough.

He didn't wait around. Rushing outside, and with a scared leap, he scampered up onto the shed's roof, crouching down like a terrified cat on top of it.

From the store, Val's voice rang out over the town.

"Nancy! Nestor!" he bellowed, waving his arms. "Get up on your roof! On your roof! They come through the floor!"

As he shouted, the noise was heard beneath. The store shuddered from the frantic movements of the creatures below the dirt. The store's floorboards cracked even more as tentacles reached up inside, searching, smashing.

"Can't you scream a little quieter?" Earl muttered out of the side of his mouth, casting a wary glance at Val.

Half a mile out of town, Burt and Heather were just pulling up to their house in their large, camo-painted Blazer.

They lived in an ugly, no-nonsense building. Made of cinder blocks and mortar, it was surrounded by a gunmetal colored chain-link fence. There was nothing homely here. No yard. No plants. Not even any paint or plaster on the outside walls. It was not welcoming, but that was the point. It was more than their home; it was their bunker. Their sanctuary.

It was a fortress. Reinforced doors, steel shutters,

and a basement stocked with enough supplies to survive an extinction-level event. But what most folks didn't know, what Burt rarely mentioned unless pressed, was that the money funding his paranoia hadn't come from any modern-day fortune. It came from deep in the past, from a rich vein of silver once mined by his great-grandfather, Hiram Gummer, back in the 1890s. The old mine, long abandoned, lay right here in the valley. That connection was what first drew Burt to Perfection. Family history within in desert stone. As the world began to feel more dangerous, Burt's sense of purpose grew louder. This place, isolated, obscure, easy to defend, seemed like the perfect spot to prepare for the end of days. Heather, his partner in arms, agreed. And so, armed with legacy and loaded magazines, they built their bunker beneath the sand.

Hot and tired, they climbed out of the Blazer, fully armed as always.

"I can't believe it," Burt sighed. "No tracks. No sign. No spoor." He wiped his brow. "You'd think after they ate all those sheep, they'd have to take a dump *some* time."

Heather, on high alert still, was not quite as resigned as Burt. She paused and turned her binoculars to the distant town of Perfection.

Burt meanwhile shuffled inside.

Through the magnified lens, she saw a surreal sight. Townsfolk scattered across rooftops like survivors in a flood. Rhonda was perched on the walkway around the head of the water tower. Val, Earl, and

Miguel were on top of Walter's store. Nancy and Mindy huddled on the roof of their house, holding each other. Nestor was on top of his trailer, and Melvin was clinging to the roof of the small rickety storage shed.

"Well, ain't that somethin'," Heather mused before shouting back to Burt. "You might wanna come back out and see this!"

Val, Earl, and Miguel looked at the town, minds racing as they tried to figure out what they could do.

Earl was the first to break their pondered silence.

"Hey, how about this," he spoke quickly, keeping his voice as quiet as possible. "Nestor's Caddy. We could sprint for it, grab the spare. Put it on our truck with our other spare as well. Tires are too small on his, but it'll do. Both flats fixed. We could drive out on that. At least to the mountains anyway."

Val stared at him, as though he had gone crazy.

"Answer me this," Val said, just as quietly. "How the hell long does it take *you* to change a tire? 'Cause I'd be out there for at least twenty minutes swapping them over. You think the worms are gonna hang fire for us to do that?"

Earl gave a long-suffering sigh. "Damn… Yeah… It'll take too damn long… Come to think of it… The bolt patterns are probably different anyway."

"We need a proper, workable plan," Val said. "There's *gotta* be a way."

Before they could think of one, the CB radio inside the store crackled to life.

'Yo, Walter,' came Burt's voice, clear and very loud. *'Burt here. Come back.'*

The building rumbled as the creatures were drawn once again by the noise.

Val, Earl, and Miguel ran to look through the ceiling hatch, eyes darting to the CB radio sat on the counter by an open window.

Val didn't hesitate. He moved across to the side of the building and looked down to where the window was.

"Grab my legs," he whispered back to Earl.

Sliding headfirst off the side, Earl and Miguel both held Val as he lowered himself off the side of the building, down to the open window where the CB radio sat buzzing loudly.

'Walter?' Burt asked loudly, not having any idea what was happening.

Val, now dangling upside down, reached out his hand and groped for the radio as the building groaned under the strain of the circling creatures below.

'Walter? Anybody copy? What's going on over there?' Burt's voice came again, louder and sounding much more annoyed.

The store shook harder as he spoke louder.

Val's fingers finally found the radio mic and yanked it free. Sticking out a thumbs up, Miguel and Earl slowly hauled him back up to the roof. The cord of the CB trailing behind him, pulling taught as Val got back on the roof.

He turned the volume down low and pressed the transmit button as he spoke into the mic in a hushed voice.

"Burt, listen," he said. "We found out what's been killing all the people."

"Say 'over,'" Earl said, elbowing him.

Val rolled his eyes and repeated, "Over."

The fortified basement of the Gummer bunker was a survivalist's dream. A meticulously organized fallout shelter nestled deep beneath their house. Wood-paneled walls gave the space a strangely cozy, almost rustic warmth. One that contrasted with the cold efficiency of its contents. High metal shelving units lined each end of the space, stacked with labeled crates, canned goods, ammunition boxes, and enough weaponry to arm a militia. Rows of military-grade MREs sat beside water purification systems as well as a line of backup generators.

A well-oiled workbench stood to one side, cluttered with tools and spare parts for everything from radios to rifles. Despite this bunker's utilitarian purpose, it was far from unwelcoming. There were creature comforts here, too: a recliner, a mounted television tuned to static, and a small shelf of dog-eared survival manuals and assorted spy themed paperbacks. Every inch of the space reflected Burt and Heather Gummer's obsession with surviving. They were people who had not only prepared for the end of the world but almost seemed to welcome it in any form.

At his desk in front of his radio, Burt looked with concern as he adjusted the frequency. Heather stood nearby at the ammunition reloading bench. Throwing a few hundred empty cartridges into a large electric cleaner and switched it on. It buzzed as it hummed to life.

"Negative copy on that, Walter, check your frequency, you're really quiet. I can't hear you." Burt checked the dial on his radio. "I'm on twenty-two. Come back."

After a few moments…. *'Burt, can you hear me now,'* Val's voice came through a bit louder.

"Only just, Walter. Now what are you all doing on your roofs? What the hell is going on over there? Come back."

Peering inside the store, Miguel stared at the groping set of tentacles that searched the shelves, keeping an eye on where they were.

As they moved around, they were almost hypnotic.

Until they stopped suddenly.

Miguel held his breath as he watched the tips all turn in one direction. The same direction. As if they could see, but it was a noise they were noticing. Something buzzing and humming far away.

In an instant, they all retracted beneath the earth.

Looking up, Miguel looked out to the town to where they were headed.

Val on the CB spoke a tiny bit louder, getting more frustrated. "It's Val, Burt. *Val.*"

"Val?" Burt said, confounded. "That you? Why are you on the radio, and what are you doing back already? Come back."

Heather peered out a narrow window slit at the top of the room toward the town.

"Something's going on there," she said. "Why the hell are they on their roofs?"

Burt shook his head, aghast.

The case cleaner rattled loudly in the background. A clanking metallic drone that neither of them seemed to notice.

Miguel pointed frantically at a pile of oil drums tipping over on the far side of the town. "They're going, man!" he whispered hoarsely. "I think they heard something…"

"Going where?" Earl replied.

"I think they're going for Burts!"

Val snatched up the CB radio, his voice louder. "Burt! Get out of your basement! Take your radio! You and Heather get up on your roof, *right now…* Then we'll talk, okay? Just get up there. Over. Over. *Over.*"

In the basement of their cinder block fortress, Burt muttered to himself. "Why the hell do I need to get on my roof? Out in the open for any enemy to see?" He then spoke into the radio again. "How about you tell me why the hell *you* all up there?" he asked, trying to understand. "Val, what the hell are you talking about? Is this a joke?"

Heather's nerves began to fray as she heard the fear in Val's voice. She grabbed Burt's arm. "Damn it, Burt. Something's wrong, can't you tell? Just listen to him!"

The CB crackled, Val's voice suddenly high and frantic. *'Burt! Burt! Jesus Christ! Get out of your basement! They're coming after you guys! They're coming right now! They can hear you!'*

Burt hesitated only for a second before the instinct for survival battled his disbelief. He and Heather quickly spun into action in what was a well-rehearsed drill. They grabbed their rifles, each moving to a narrow window on opposite sides of the room. Both with binoculars in hand, they looked out into the desert. Surveying the land beyond for any sign of an enemy.

But there was nothing out there but sand.

"Negative North, Northwest," he said in military form.

He glanced over at Heather. She shook her head.

"Negative north, northeast."

Burt shook his head. "If whatever it is, is coming at us from the town, we would have seen it by now," he said. "This better not be a prank." He picked up the radio again. "We don't see anything coming this way, Val. Now tell me what the hell are you talking about? Come back."

Up on Walter's roof, Val was nearly jumping out of his skin, shouting back through the radio, "The things! They're under the ground! They're huge! They dig! Big damn slimy snake monsters! Now get the hell up! Hurry! Hurry! Hurry!"

Burt lowered the binoculars, smiling to hide his anger. He turned to Heather, about to unleash a tirade about how unfunny this was, that people and animals were dead, and that this was no time for jokes. But before he could utter a word, they both felt it: a low, deep vibration coming from all around them, something that shook the very foundations of this bunker.

The tools hanging on the pegboard over the workbenches rattled. The television mounted on the walls clattered on its mounting. Even the overhead strip lights swayed on their suspension wires.

Everything soon settled again, and the room went still for a few heartbeats. Burt and Heather stared at each other, neither knowing what had just happened.

"You think they finally did it?" Heather asked.

Burt shrugged. "Only a matter of time before someone pushed the damn button… Still doesn't explain why they're on the roofs."

The quiet split in an instant as the wall behind them cracked inward with the deafening sound of concrete splitting. Hairline fractures spidered out in every direction, as the paneling that lined the walls split open. The metal rack shuddered as it snapped off its bearings, toppling and clattering its tools loudly across the stone floor. A trophy cow skull, bleached and mounted above the shelves, fell too, shattering as it landed. Jagged bone and metal lay in front of Burt and Heather, where they stared in total shock.

Neither of them had time to chamber a round as the wall then exploded. Cinder blocks and rebar shot out like shrapnel. With a furious roar, a Graboid smashed through, with half of its revolting, slimy body surging into the basement like a living battering ram. Its armored hide glistened with grime, streaked with dirt. Its bony jaws opened wide, revealing concentric circles of glistening teeth reaching all the way down its endless gullet, as writhing, flailing tentacles reached out to them. Lashing wildly, wrapping around anything they could grab. Shelving fell, cases of ammunition were knocking over, crates of survival gear were sent crashing to the floor.

As it roared at them once more, its rotten boiling breath blasted into the room.

• • •

On Walter's rooftop, Val, Earl, and Miguel huddled around the CB, eyes staring at the speaker, waiting. Hoping for a reply. The static on the line crackled then came a sound. A short, sharp click, as the CB went dead.

No one spoke. They stared at each other in a numb horror. Then, faintly, drifting over the still desert, came the unmistakable *pop-pop-pop* of gunfire. Short bursts at first, then a rolling cacophony of munitions being unleashed.

In the basement, the sound was overwhelming and deafening. Like a full-scale war being in this small basement.

Burt and Heather stood, semi-automatic rifles in hand, firing in tandem, their training turning any fear they may have deep inside, into a focused and unrelenting assault.

Muzzle flashes lit the room in strobing pulses. Rounds slammed into the Graboid, some pinging off its armored beak, but others shot through softer, more vulnerable sections of its mouth and down in its cavernous throat. The beast recoiled, shrieking, as foul orange blood sprayed in thick waves that painted the basement and them.

Heather side-stepped one torrent of goo, as she reloaded her rifle, eyes never leaving the creature once. Burt, meanwhile, cursed under his breath, yanking a fresh magazine from his belt as one torrent hit him in the chest.

The monster bellowed again, its entire bulk writhing through the breach, bringing down more of the wall with it. Trying to get in. Trying to get to them.

As it did, the whole room, and the house above, shook down to its moorings.

Suddenly, a tentacle shot out from its mouth like a whip, wrapping around Burt's ankle. With a jerk, it pulled him off his feet, slamming him to the side, hard into a high stack of provisions. Cans were thrown to the floor, bursting open, scattering their emergency rations of beans and peaches, but worst of all, the rifle had been knocked out of his hands, and clattered in a pool of goo a few feet away.

Heather didn't hesitate. She swung her rifle around, pivoted her aim to the tentacle pulling at Burt, and fired. The flurry of bullets blasted the tentacle clean in half, monster blood spraying over Burt's face. He quickly got to his feet again and offered a single nod of appreciation to his wife, taking off his gloop-covered glasses.

Another tentacle swung at him, but he was ready. Without time to grab his fallen rifle, he snatched a hatchet off the bench and brought it down with a grunt, severing the appendage in one brutal chop.

They were not even close to being beaten.

They attacked fast and adrenaline-fueled.

A long procession of weapons came out and took their turns. Revolvers, lever-action rifles, sawed-off shotguns… they grabbed and used whatever was within reach.

Heather spotted the flare gun and without thinking grabbed it and fired straight into the monster's mouth. It rocketed from the gun, flew straight past the tentacles and vanished down its fleshy gullet.

Burt could not help but grin as he saw it, adding to the shots by firing a short-barreled M1 at point-blank range.

Then the creature let out an almighty roar. An unearthly, metallic scream as smoke from the flare started to pour out over its jaws. As it did, its whole body convulsed. Slamming from side to side into the concrete floor with a seismic force, not understanding what was now happening inside it.

As it thrashed, it sent huge shockwaves through the house, nearly toppling both Burt and Heather off their feet… But that didn't stop it trying to lurch forward to them.

Both retreated, step by step, back to the gun wall, as the creature forced its way further through the crack in the wall, rage and agony from the flare making it more ferocious.

One of the tentacles lashed inches away from Heather's face, as she ducked, then came up with a pump-action shotgun. Stepping closer, she aimed straight at its mouth and pulled the trigger. The tentacle's flesh broke apart as gore sprayed out covering her. But she didn't mind. It was part of the battle.

With no room left to backpedal, and his guns out of

bullets, Burt turned. He had one big card left to play. With his elbow he shattered a locked glass cabinet that sat below the window. From inside, he pulled out a four-gauge elephant gun. A huge gun. Cocking its wide barrels, he took two brass shells that sat in the cabinet. Two shells that were the size of carrots. He shoved them into the breach. As he did, Heather was covering him, blasting the creature again and again with two revolvers, keeping it at bay.

Burt could not hide his glee, as he stepped forward, leveling the elephant gun aimed at the advancing creature.

He fired.

The recoil sent him hurtling backward, slamming into the gun wall.

The Graboid reeled, its front half now a cavernous gorge that exploded in a wash of steaming blood and shredded cartilage. Its shrieks were more gurgles, and it didn't advance any more, convulsing as if life had been blasted out of it.

It collapsed forward, as its insides came pouring through the wounds, onto the floor toward them. Coating their shoes.

But it somehow still wasn't *quite* dead.

It twitched. A final desperate lurch.

Burt cocked the gun again. The second shell went in.

He grimaced as he aimed.

BOOM.

This time, the Graboid could not survive. The blast

ripped through what remained of its head. Fragments of bone, muscle, and mandible sprayed like shrapnel across the basement.

Seeing this defeat, Burt dropped to one knee, chest heaving, sweat dripping off his brow. He gripped the elephant gun like a battle flag. Heather lowered her weapon and let out a long breath, eyes still fixed on the smoking corpse, just in case.

Slowly got back up, Burt felt his veins bulge in his neck as he screamed at the deflated, disemboweled beast. "You broke into the *wrong* Goddamn rec room, didn't you, you bastard!"

Heather wiped her face, glancing around at the wreckage. Half of their arsenal and provisions were destroyed… But they were both alive. And that *thing* sure as hell wasn't.

Val, Earl, and Miguel sat motionless, still staring at the CB, waiting. Then, through the static, Burt's triumphant voice cracked through:

'We killed it! You got that? We killed that motherfucker! Come back! We won the war!'

The men let out a whispered cheer, punching the air with fists.

Val clicked the transmitter. "Uh…roger that, Burt. Uh, congratulations? But… You gotta know, there are two more, repeat, two more motherfuckers out there. You only killed one motherfucker. Come back."

• • •

In Burt and Heather's basement, the two survivalists didn't celebrate for too long. The euphoria of their underground victory was brief, evaporating the moment Val let them in on the facts. As soon as they understood, they swung into action. They grabbed crates of weapons, ammunition, provisions and other necessities for war. Heather yanked the CB radio from its mount, wrapping the cord hastily around its base as Burt unlocked their backup weapons locker, removing even more high-powered munitions.

They dashed outside and clambered up the steel ladder to their flat concrete roof, hauling the crates with them. They ran back and forth until everything they needed for a fight was up there ready.

Once they had set up, they hit the deck, laying low against the sun-heated concrete. Heather swung open the lid of a weapons case and pulled free a scoped semi-automatic. Burt, ever the one for overkill, crouched beside an identical weapon, as well as the massive elephant gun, not to mention boxes and boxes of ammunition at the ready.

Their next action was to survey the land. Scopes swept back and forth across the open terrain, searching for any stirrings in the ground. Signs of movement from underneath.

The battle was far from over, but Burt and Heather Gummer were ready.

Chapter 7

Making Plans

Val edged to the roof's side. "Burt and Heather got one," he shouted. "They killed one of those sons of bitches."

On the rickety storage shed, Melvin pumped his fist in the air. "Way to go, dudes!" he cried out over-enthusiastically.

On the Sterngood roof, Nancy and Mindy smiled happily, still hugging each other.

On his trailer roof, Nestor poured a cup of coffee from his thermos and raised it up in a silent toast.

From the water tower, Rhonda let out a "Whoop!"

But Val should have known better than to shout anything, as the ground shifted below the shattered siding beneath him.

He looked shocked, presuming the worms had left to go to Burt's, but were obviously back here.

Earl whispered. "I guess we can't make fun of Burt's lifestyle anymore, huh? He was prepared. We weren't."

Val quietly stepped over to the CB and clicked on the mic. "Burt, it's Val," he whispered. "Any chance you can get the rest of them with what you got? You got enough guns?"

"One second, Val," Burt replied as he stared out to the ground below, where he could see the earth bulging upward against the house's foundation.

Grabbing his elephant gun, he loaded both barrels, stood and aimed downward.

Boom!

Boom!

He took two well aimed shots, having braced himself enough that the recoil didn't send him flying.

The noise echoed around the surrounding mountains, but the bullets themselves landed in the sand without doing much harm at all.

The bulge in the dirt calmly moved away and sunk deeper as it did.

Burt looked disappointed.

"You're not getting any penetration, even with the elephant gun." Heather said.

"Damn," Burt nodded in agreement, as he picked up the CB again. "Val, we're gonna have to get them to breach. Can't shoot them in the dirt. Best Goddamn bullet in the world wouldn't reach them down there. But what I got will get them if they poke their heads out. I think. This one took so much ammo, but we may have been just lucky."

Val and Miguel look disappointed, not getting the answer they expected from Burt.

With a sudden idea, Earl took the CB and spoke quietly into it. "Burt, it's Earl. Now listen, forget about shooting them. Tell me this, can you get to your truck?"

'Sure, I can, no problem… Why?'

"Good. You've got the only vehicle in the valley that can make it up the old jeep trail. So, here's a plan: you and Heather go for help. Go via the mountains—"

From over at the water tower, Rhonda called out. Pointing down at the base of Walter's store. "Guys! Hey, guys! Look, they're up to something!"

The three men carefully looked over to the side of the store, down to where she was pointing.

Sure enough below, a creature was now poking its tentacles out of the sand, running them along the building's base.

"Hey look," Val said, pointing to a half torn off tentacle. "It's that one again. Think I'll call him Axle."

Earl stared at the tentacles. "Bastard took Walter," he seethed. He turned to Rhonda. "What's it doing?"

"Why do you all keep asking *me*?" she called back. "I'm studying seismology, not monsters!"

They all watched, nervous in the heat as the creature felt along the entire edge of the building, each tentacle feeling out the clapboard, piece by piece, like it was reading braille. It slid along the wall until it reached the corner, then dipped out of sight, drawing its feelers back in as it submerged back underground.

They all stared, waiting for the monster to come back up and feel around the next side. But instead, one entire side of Chang's store suddenly lifted off the ground.

Wood splintered loudly, as one closed window shattered, the clapboard splitting as the corner of the building rose upward by a clear two feet. The whole rooftop tilted under their feet. They were barely able to keep their balance as they stumbled back. Then, just as quickly as it rose, the building dropped back down.

"What the hell was that all about?" Earl said.

The CB crackled beside him.

'Breaker there, Earl,' Burt's voice came through. *'What do you want us to do again? Come back?'*

Earl picked up the handset, eyes still on the dirt. "Hang on, Burt. This bastard's trying something new."

Across the street, Nancy and Mindy clung to each other on their roof. Just like at Walter's something deep below began to push against the foundations below them.

The groan of the house's frame was soft at first, almost like a groan from an old man trying to stand. But then it came on louder. And with those groans came the cracking of wooden beams.

Nancy and Mindy closed their eyes tight, as tight as their grip to each other was. Somewhere inside the kitchen beneath, dishes fell from a shelf and shattered on the floor. The house was tilting at an angle, threatening collapse. Inside anything that wasn't held down was falling and sliding. Crashing and smashing.

Mindy cried out as she started to slip back, as the roof slanted. Whatever was beneath them was pushing it up further and further, much higher than it did the store. Nancy reached out, grabbing her daughter just in time before she could tumble off the side and to the ground below where the monsters waited. Mindy clung on, tears streaming, until the upward motion slowed, and the house settled back down again.

The men watched Nancy's house confused and angry.

"They weren't making no damn noise?" Miguel said angrily. "What are those things bothering them for? How do they even know they're there?"

"Maybe they are just studying the buildings?" Val said, grasping at straws. "Trying to figure 'em out or somethin'? Who knows, maybe they've never even seen a house before?"

From the water tower, Rhonda shouted over. "They're confused."

Earl looked at her. "Huh, what?"

"*Confused*," she reiterated. "They must be able to feel that there are vibrations up here, but when they come up, they only find solid buildings. They can't find us, and they can't understand why."

"Maybe," Earl replied. "But it looks to me like

they're coming up with some sort of plan. Like they know exactly what is goin' on."

The creatures soon turned their attention to Nestor's trailer.

It began with a sound.

Not a growl or a groan as before. Not even a rumble. Just a low, slow creak, like the metal of his trailer was beginning to stretch. Nestor, with a look of shock from all he'd seen still on his face, sat in a battered lawn chair on his roof. He shouted as the floor beneath him started to move to one side. The whole trailer then trembled, not much, but just enough to make the coffee in his mug ripple.

He sat up straighter, wiping his eyes, forcing himself fully alert.

The trailer then lifted up, followed by another tremble. This one was more violent. One that caused the chair to skid a few inches to the left.

Then the whole place jolted. A sudden wail of steel twisted, brought to breaking point, as Nestor felt the whole trailer lift slightly.

"Oh, what the hell…?" he gasped, pushing off his chair, keeping his balance as he turned.

Then everything happened at once.

WHAM, the ground beneath the trailer gave a monstrous heave, as the entire home lifted at one end faster and more forcefully than it had done previously.

Nestor yelled out, looking to grab onto something, anything to help him remain on top.

The sound of the creature huffing could be heard as it sank quickly then hit from beneath a second time. *WHAM*, and it was this impact that sent Nestor careening off from the safety of the trailer and landed with a thud on the sandy dirt below.

As he landed, the rest of what he had on the roof came down too, raining around him. A toolbox pitched and burst open by his legs. Nails and screws and socket wrenches everywhere. His open thermos landed a few feet away, spraying its contents all over him. The lawn chair a few feet beyond them.

The trailer lowered quickly, then *WHAM!* Another colossal from underneath. Much harder. It seemed as if the whole vehicle had been uppercut by a wrecking ball.

The huffing and snorting sound of the creature got louder as it moved to one side. And as it did, the whole building skidded sideways with it.

Nestor scrambled, crawling to a huge rubber tire that sat near his house. Three feet thick, and something he was now glad he didn't get scrapped. He's had plans to grow something in it, to make it a feature outside his trailer, but right now, he was just relieved it was there.

He scrambled up onto it, pulling himself onto the rim as if onto a life raft. He lay across the tire's large hole, with his shoulder on one edge and his legs on the other. He immediately forced himself to be quiet. Stilling his breathing as much as possible. Keeping his fear inside.

But his panting was louder than he thought it was. With every rise and fall of his chest, a small vibration coursed through the tire. Though rubber was a natural dampener for such things, whatever was below could sense even the slightest movement even through that.

As he closed his eyes and imagined being on a beach, somewhere far away, somewhere safe, he forced his mind from this terrifying moment....

In an instant, two tentacles shot up through the middle of the tire, rising on either side of him. They immediately wrapped around his belly, knocking all breath out. They then yanked him down through the tire's hole.

Without time to react, his body folded in half at the spine, snapping it instantly, and he was pulled down into the dirt.

It was so sudden, his screams were taken down with him. Sounding only for a few seconds as they got deeper, fainter and more muffled until finally, there was silence.

But under the dirt, the scream continued. Dull. Distant. Going deeper and deeper and deeper. Until finally, it was gone.

Across the street in the storage shed, Melvin rocked back and forth slowly on the roof. Knees hugged to his chest, arms wrapped around them. He had seen and heard everything that happened to Nestor, and now all his bravado and cockiness were gone.

"Oh, man," he whispered through horrified tears. "No way. No frickin' way, man..."

Across the street, having seen Nestor's demise too, Nancy held onto Mindy even tighter, as the child trembled in her arms. Nancy pressed her cheek to her daughter's head, whispering.

"It'll be alright. I promise. It'll be alright."

Up on the water tower, Rhonda had turned her face away, not wanting to see what became of Nestor. As soon as he had hit the dirt, she knew what would happen, what the Graboid intended. She could not do a thing to help, but also did not want his final moment to be part of her memory.

Back on top of Chang's, Miguel made the sign of the cross, fingers trembling as he tapped his shoulders, chest and head. He, Val and Earl stared in disbelief at the trailer, now on one side. They saw it too, as helpless as everyone else.

"It's figured out where we are," Miguel said. "It can get us no matter how silent we try to be."

No one argued, it was all so very clear.

Earl nodded. "They're gonna tear all these buildings down 'til we're dead."

Val rushed back onto the CB radio.

Burt and Heather were still on their roof.

Heather sat by the CB, as Burt patrolled the cinderblock ramparts. With his elephant gun in hand, he had a smile on his face. This may have been a war, but that didn't mean Burt couldn't enjoy himself. He stared out around his modest compound. Fence, check. Truck, check. Expanse of desert, check. Not that there was much else to check on.

'Burt! Heather! Come in.' Val's voice came over the CB, as hushed as ever.

Heather picked up the receiver. "Ten-four Val. You're a go for Heather. Come back."

'We're in kinda deep shit over here. They got Nestor and are trying to bring the buildings down. We need to change plans!'

"We haven't even got to our truck yet," she said. "We're gonna go in five when the coast is clear. We still got movement."

Burt wasn't listening to the conversation. He was busy staring down from the wall, at the patch of ground near the base of the house where he had seen a hump of dirt rise and fall.

Then it moved again.

With a gritting of teeth, Burt aimed the elephant gun down off the roof and fired. It boomed loudly. As the bullet smacked onto the dirt below, the hump of dirt turned and moved away, passing under a concrete sidewalk that surrounded the property. The flagstones gently rippled as it went by.

"Knock it off, Burt," Heather complained. "It's a waste of ammo if it can't hit it."

But Burt was feeling happy staring at the hump of dirt getting further out.

"I think I scared it," he said.

'Forget going for help,' Val continued over the radio. *'We'll all be dead here long before you reach anyone.'*

"We're here for you, Val," Heather said into the radio. "Just tell us what you need. Come back."

'The one here is gonna tear this town out from underneath us. It's hitting the bottom of each building. We all gotta get out of here together. Now! Over. Can you come get us?'

"Roger that, Val," Heather replied. "We'll come get everybody. Just hang—"

The Blazer's security alarm started wailing. Heather immediately got to her feet and rushed over beside Burt.

As the vehicle's siren sounded loudly, it was helpless as a large Graboid breached the dirt beside it. Its tentacles lashing at the chassis furiously. The metal ripped with ease as the tires were shredded.

Burt stared as his beloved truck was obliterated right before his eyes. He almost cried, as if he were watching a family member perish. He let out a soft, sad whine, which Heather could hear despite the cacophony of the Graboid attack. She placed a comforting hand on his shoulder.

The truck alarm sounded across the valley, whining in a waving tone, before choking off with a final sputter. Val, Earl, and Miguel stared into the emptiness, in the direction of the Gummer's house.

Heather's voice crackled over the CB radio.

'Val, we're gonna have to forget about the truck...'

Val lifted the radio to his mouth, his voice dull and resigned to their bad luck. "Yeah, Heather, we figured."

They had hit another wall, and not for the first time today.

Earl looked perturbed by something else. "We say we needed a truck, those Graboids take the truck." He looked at Val. "You don't think they knew, do you?"

"You think they hear us? And understand?" Miguel asked.

Earl shrugged. "Maybe, we know shit about shit here."

Up on the roof of the nearby storage shed, Melvin had begun to panic more and more. He stood up and was pacing in tight circles on the small sheet of corrugated iron roof, his fists clenched.

"Hey," he called out. "You all better think of something soon, man! You gotta do something!"

Earl looked blankly at him. "Who better?" he called back.

"You and Val, man!" came the reply.

Miguel nodded in agreement.

That was enough to set Val off. "What?" he shouted. "Since when the hell's every Goddamn thing up to us? Why?"

"Shhh, keep it down," Earl cut in.

Rhonda had heard and added from her place on the water tower. "You guys do all the odd jobs," she said. "And this whole thing is damn odd."

Val turned to her, staring as if waiting for her to laugh. She didn't.

Then came a *crash*. Something massive slammed into the side of the store. The creature was back and gave the building a full-bodied assault. The store groaned as it started to lean. One corner lifted clean off the ground as the monster pressed up from underneath. It hung there for a moment before crashing back down. The porch in front collapsed with a splintering crack, and then the real attack began.

The monster was pounding, ramming, grinding as hard and fast as it could across the entire base of the building. And as it did, the earth below became looser and looser. The whole store lost its footing and started to sink down. The whole building rocked as if it was in the epicenter of a megaquake.

"We don't have a hell of a lot of time here," Earl shouted out. No longer concerned with keeping quiet.

Rhonda shouted over. "Look, the situation hasn't changed. We still have to get to solid rock. There must be *some* way, *some*thing we can do. You know this place."

Miguel, meanwhile, was thinking about what was said. He leaned over the side. "Hey, Graboid, if you let us all go we will get you all the food you need!" He turned to Earl who was looking at him quizzically. "As you said, we know shit about shit."

Val was incensed about everyone relying on them to fix it all. The fear in his gut had turned to anger. He screamed at the whole town. "And what are we gonna do, huh? There's nothing left that'll make it up to the mountains! You think I can pull us a damn truck out of my ass just 'cause we need it? Magic up a helicopter?"

"Hey, Val, quiet it down, man, they could be listening." Miguel warned, flinching as the structure took another massive hit, as one corner of the building dipped down.

"It don't matter now," Earl said to Miguel. "They know full well where we are."

Val pressed on, almost talking to himself. "We need a tank is what we need… Or a flock of damn eagles to carry us there!"

Earl stopped. A smile appeared on his previously miserable face. "Wait one minute," he said. "What about the Cat? Could we take the Cat?"

Val hesitated before answering, looking at Earl as if he'd lost his mind. "Jesus. It's slower than hell. We may as well walk!"

"Yeah, I know it's slow, but it weighs better than thirty tons. No way those things could lift thirty tons… could they? I mean—"

"Earl," Miguel interjected. "We can't *all* fit on that bulldozer."

Val was deep in thought. The idea now didn't seem too dumb after all. "You're right. They are frickin' massive, but the Cat is too big and heavy. And for getting everyone… we could pull something. We could drag a car behind it."

"They attack cars," Miguel shook his head.

"Ok, not a car." Earl scratched his chin. "What about a truck? Nah. Need something bigger. Tougher. Something they would have a problem with…" He thought more as he looked out over the side to a discarded mobile home. "Or, hell, that old semi-trailer."

"The tires are flat," Val pointed out.

"How does that matter," Earl said. "The Cat can pull *any*thing."

They looked at each other, wondering if this was the answer they were looking for, or a suicide mission waiting to happen.

Val nodded. "Well… all right, my friends. That is how we'll roll on out of here."

"We got ourselves a plan," Earl grinned.

"What about the keys?" Miguel asked.

"Nestor insisted they stay in the Cat at all times."

Earl smirked. "It was after you lost the first set."

"Potayto Potahto," Val replied.

They all turned, squinting into the distance as the sun shone just above where the machine sat. The Cat. The bulldozer. It was to the west of town. Still intact.

"'Course, that's one helluva long walk," Earl added. "How do we get there?"

They stared, momentarily stuck in the problem.

Rhonda spoke up.

"Listen. They only respond to vibrations we make, right?"

"And?" Earl replied.

"Well, couldn't we distract them somehow?"

Val's eyes lit up. "Yeah, good. Something to keep them busy. We need a decoy…" he turned to Miguel and Earl. "But who?"

Earl held in a chuckle as he turned and looked over to the small storage shed. "Hey, Melvin," he shouted. "You wanna make yourself a buck?"

"Screw you!" Melvin replied. Not missing a beat, even though he had no idea what was being asked of him.

Miguel pulled at Earl's arm and pointed him to a pile of old equipment at the far side of the store. There, buried among rusted tools, weeds and tangled hose, sat a small tractor.

"How about that?" Miguel said. "Walter's little tractor? Still works. Saw him on it last week. Just need to start it up, let it go off by itself. Let those things chase it all over if they like the noise. Don't even have to risk our lives trying to lure 'em away."

Earl gave an approving nod. "Not bad." He turned to Val. "What do you think?"

The store then took another heavy hit from below. One corner cracked inward, sagging the roof at an angle. The three men grabbed onto the ledge behind them, stopping them falling.

"Damn, we *should* still be quiet," Earl chastised himself.

Val looked at the shaking and sinking roof. "I say we go right now."

Rhonda shouted out. "Wait. How are you going to know if anything's following it? There's two of them?"

Val paused. "Good point."

Earl looked down at the roof below. "We got one right here."

Val got to his feet and stood on the highest point of the buckling roof.

"Melvin! Nancy! Can you see where the other bastard is?"

Nancy's house was shuddering and shaking. It wasn't even a question she had to think about answering. She held her daughter close and cried out. "Here! It's right *here!*"

CHAPTER 8

THE LAST STAND

Melvin watched from the roof of the storage shed. His face, usually sneering or smug, had turned pale. He was not holding himself together at all.

At the front of Chang's store, Val and Earl were leaning over the edge of the now semi-collapsed roof, muscles tensed as they lowered Miguel on a loop of coax cable that had ripped off the television antennae. He dangled off the side, down to the narrow ledge that sat above the garden tractor.

Nervous and overheated, sweat soaked his shirt and dripped onto the tractor.

"He sure doesn't look this heavy," Earl muttered to Val as they strained holding the cord.

Finally, Miguel managed to plant his boots steady: one on the windowsill and one on the tractor's seat.

He untied the kerchief around his neck and reached out to the controls. Looping the fabric through the steering wheel, he tied it against the gear stick, stopping the wheel from being able to turn too far off course.

After jamming the throttle open, he threw a trembling thumbs up to the men above. He kept his gaze level, fully expecting the ground to explode at any moment.

With Miguel's cord lying on the end of the roof, Val and Earl had already moved, striding to the other side. Their steps as quiet as possible.

It didn't take long for them to realize they both had the same idea.

"What the hell are you doing?" Earl asked.

"I'm making the run to the Cat," Val said matter-of-factly.

"Like hell you are," Earl dismissed, edging a step ahead.

"Get real, I'm way faster than you, old man."

"Old?" Earl stopped and faced him. "Well, I'm better at driving the Cat, *kid*."

Val scoffed. "Better than Melvin, sure. But not me."

Earl pointed a finger at Val's chest. "Look, you'd better listen. I'm older, yeah, but I'm also wiser."

"Yeah, well you're half right there."

Without another word, Earl raised a fist up to Val's face.

The Challenge. The time-honored method of decision.

Rock. Paper. Scissors.

One, two, three.

Val threw scissors. Earl threw rock.

"Damnit, you won," Val said with a sigh. "Guess I have to do it then."

He went to walk away, but Earl stopped him.

"Hey, I won," he said firmly. "*I* pick who does it."

Val stopped, glaring. But Earl's face was set like stone, and as determined as he ever had been before.

"Ready when you are, Miguel," Earl shouted out, not breaking eye contact with Val.

Tuning he then positioned himself, allowing his nerves to show as he looked at the Cat.

From below, Miguel leaned precariously over the tractor and yanked at the pull cord.

The tractor sputtered once, then died.

"Hijo de puta," Miguel moaned, before reaching for the cord again and pulling at it harder.

It caught.

The engine roared to life, coughing smoke as it did. Miguel stepped off the seat and back onto the windowsill. When he had a firm grip he kicked out at the tractor's gear stick, throwing it into drive, and watched as it trundled forward. Through the weeds and out onto the open road. The engine rumbling loudly as it did.

The entire store shuddered beneath Miguel as something massive peeled away from far below, chasing the sound that was now headed on the road out of town.

"There he goes!" Miguel shouted. "He's chasing it!"

· · ·

On Nancy's rooftop, a thick spout of dust erupted near her house's foundation, blasting upward in a plume as the creature shifted direction, turning and leaving them in silence.

Nancy's voice was barely a whisper. "It's going…" she said. Then louder, she cried a triumphant yell: "There goes this one! It's coming!"

On the store roof, Earl crouched, ready to leap. But Val was suddenly beside him, a grin on his face as he slapped Earl hard on the back.

"Hey, watch your ass, shithead."

Earl smirked, liking the idea that they could do this together. "Don't worry about me, jerk off, just stay alive."

But Val wasn't thinking that at all. He quickly elbowed Earl hard in the gut, backed up two steps and sprang clean off the roof. Leaving Earl doubled over, grunting.

"You suicidal son of a bitch!" Earl wheezed.

Val had hit the dirt running, and he didn't look back once.

The bulldozer, the Cat, sat on the far side of town. Nestor's prized bulldozer. Never left at the dump when not in use, he had always wanted to keep an eye on it. So, it always kept just on the edge of town where he could see it from his trailer's window.

Where it was, it basked in the heat, sunlight glinting off its old metal. And to Val, though it was a long way away, it somehow seemed to be getting farther with every desperate stride that he took.

His initial smile had faded, as his legs started to ache, and his lungs started to tighten.

Headed the other way, the garden tractor bounced and rattled over the desert floor as it got beyond the last building. Its engine sounded like a banshee, straining due to its age, but still working.

Val thundered across the flats, his boots hammering loudly on the dirt. His lungs were burning, each breath a struggle. All he could think of was, if he was like this now, how bad would Earl have been. That man drank more beer, smoked more cigarettes and did a lot less exercise than anyone he knew.

Then all Val could think of was how he could actually do with a beer and a smoke right now.

The tractor front tires hit a divot, a rut hidden in its path under a collection brush. The wheel bounced once, as the tractor shook from side to side. When the back wheels hit the divot, it was game over, the whole tractor flipped over onto its side.

It landed with a thud, as the engine cut out and the rattle in its body fell quiet.

Having been pulled back onto the roof by Earl, Miguel stared at the fallen tractor.

"Mierda," Miguel said.

"Oh, for the love of God, really?" Earl looked annoyed as he peered up at the sky above. "Cut us some slack for once!"

Val's boots were incredibly loud on the gravel. Even louder now the tractor was not there to mask his noise. Something Val only just realized.

He skidded to a stop mid-run, turned and looked back.

He was exposed. Alone. Running in cowboy boots on an open stretch of land. Halfway between the store and the dozer.

"Damn," he grimaced as he turned back to the bulldozer and ran again. This time having the added focus: if the tractor was dead, then all the Graboids would hear his running.

He ran faster than he'd ever done in his life.

As he pushed himself to the limit, the desert blurred around him. He moved his legs so fast it felt like his feet barely touched the ground. He wasn't thinking of anything anymore, he was just moving in a blind panic.

He wasn't alone.

Behind him, as the tractor's engine failed, the monsters *had* heard him and were on their way.

From high up, everyone could see as two enormous masses rippled through the earth. The dirt cracking above them as they burrowed in Val's direction.

"He'll never make it," Earl said in shock. "They're gonna get him."

"*Val! Stop!*" Rhonda screamed. "*They're coming, don't move, stay still!*"

Her voice carried down through the town like a thunderclap, and Val heard.

He skidded to a sudden stop. Grit flew up from around his boots. Everything within him screamed to keep going, to keep running. But he stayed still. He closed his eyes and prayed that this was the right move. If not, it would be his last.

Ten feet behind him, the desert broke apart.

Twin snouts burst up through the ground like whales breaching the sea. Their slimy skin glistened in the light as their bony jaws opened. Tentacles writhed and flailed, hunting blindly, searching, tasting the air. Waiting to hear any noise to guide them.

Val stood still, sweat pouring down his back.

One tentacle brushed closer, near to his boot.

Closer, closer—

He lifted his foot with delicate precision, balancing on one leg as it passed by.

It soon retracted and tried another path.

Too nervous to put his boot back down, he stood

there like a flamingo, staring at the two creatures desperately wanting to eat him.

Up on the store, Earl let out a breath of relief. "It's working," he said. "They can't see him."

He paused, then looked at Miguel and to Rhonda.

"Okay, okay... we gotta make noise. A *lot* of noise, you get me?"

He turned to the Graboids and bellowed: "Hey you sorry sons of bitches, come and get *my* ass!"

"Hey, ven a buscarme, estúpido!" Miguel joined in, speaking in Spanish. Stomping his foot as he did, making as much noise as possible.

From the storage shed roof, Melvin added his own hollers, half-brave, half-scared shitless, but every voice helped. "Hey, you wormy assholes! Hey! *Hey!*"

Rhonda joined in too. Hollering a series of *whoops* and *heys.* She soon realized they needed something louder. Looking around she spotted a rusted tap that stuck out from the old water tank. Turning to it, she braced herself on the guard rail, lifted her foot and kicked at the tap as hard as she could.

The pipe groaned, clanked and shuddered with each kick. Finally on the fourth try, it tore free with a sharp *crack,* breaking loose at its brittle joint.

As it came away, a torrent of water quickly followed. Blasting out from the pressure, thundering down to the dirt below.

At the end of town, the Graboid's snouts turned. Tentacles hesitating as they all pointed in the direction of the water tower. Then slowly, they sank back down into the holes they had come out from.

Val stood staring at the ground, still on one foot, as he watched the cracks trailing off back to town.

He gasped with relief, and though his lungs still burned, he pushed forward. The bulldozer ahead like a big, ugly savior.

Back at the water tower, the frenzy was rising. The gushing torrent had pooled into a shallow basin below, and now tentacles thrashed up through it, blind and desperate as it looked for the source of the noise. Mud started to build, and water flew in all directions as the monsters clawed around the expanding pool.

Rhonda recoiled, hugging the tank as the spray of water was thrown up by the thrashing beasts.

"That did it, girl!" Earl shouted from the store. "Goddamn good thinking!"

Rhonda didn't answer, she just kept her eyes on Val, as he was now climbing into the bulldozer.

· · ·

Landing in the worn driver's seat of the big machine, Val didn't waste any time as he turned the key.

The engine coughed loudly as, with a roar of grinding metal, the Cat came to sudden life. A cloud of black smoke jettisoned from its exhaust, clearing its mechanical throat as it rumbled loudly.

Val let out a loud "Woohoo," as he jammed the gears into reverse and rolled backward. The heavy treads dug deep furrows in the sand as the behemoth moved back in the direction of the rusted-out semi-trailer that lay about two hundred yards away.

The tentacles thrashing up through the water were getting more furious, as the tap still poured down onto them.

"They're damn scary, but boy they're dumb" Earl laughed to Miguel, who did not share in the humor.

"Shh, they might hear you," Miguel said, still worried about the possibility.

Back at the Cat, with its engine still ticking over, Val leapt down from the seat, hurriedly made his way to the rear of the machine and hauled out the thick, grease-streaked chain that hung there. He dragged it, grunting under its weight, to the front of the old trailer now a few feet behind him.

Reaching the front end, he crouched and secured

the chain to its tow bar. Once everything was locked in place, he gave the chain as a firm tug as he could.

Climbing into its cab again, he grasped the controls, threw it into drive and shoved his foot down onto the gas pedal. The engine roared as the bulldozer jolted forward, straining against the weight behind it.

The strain only lasted a second though, as the trailer was soon ripped clear of its mooring. The tires cracked and split away from the base, but then it was soon free and being pulled with ease across the sand.

The bulldozer plowed forward, roaring down the road, towing the trailer behind.

Val could not hide his joy.

As the bulldozer rumbled into view, it headed first to the water tower.

Its large scoop rose in the air to meet Rhonda.

But the tank was starting to groan loudly.

The rusted beams of the old tower were creaking, bending at their joints as the soil below began to shift violently, and the concrete supports were getting moved from below. As the thrashing of tentacles below churned the mud into something close to quicksand, and the Graboid's body slammed against the supports, one thing was certain.... The tower was coming down.

Rhonda clung to the guardrail as she braced her legs wide, boots pressed against the metal of the catwalk. The entire structure gave a loud metallic moan as it lurched slowly to the side.

"Val!" she screamed, but the sound was drowned in the roar of the Cat's engine.

Val saw it happening: the tower tipping, Rhonda hanging on, the weight of the tank pulling everything to one side.

"*Shit!*" he spat and jammed the throttle. The bulldozer surged forward, gears grinding as he raised the scoop as high as it would go.

The tower gave one last groan as two supports below shifted once more, and the other two sunk deeper into the mud.

Then, with a shriek of tearing bolts, it began to fall.

Rhonda screamed. A split-second of weightless terror as she felt the world give way. The tank broke loose in a twist of steel, water and sky.

But just as she dropped…

…The dozer scoop caught her.

She crashed into the raised bucket, stopping her fall, as the tower crashed into the side of Chang's store, crushing into the wall. The galvanized tank split open like a soda can, unleashing a torrent of high-pressure water that gushed across the remnants of the store in a flash flood. The wall of water came with a deafening roar.

One side of the structure caved inward as windows exploded, shelves toppled, and a gaping hole was ripped open in the side facing the street.

Mud, debris, and debris-laden water surged in like a river.

Earl and Miguel had to scamper to the other side of the roof as the water burst, shaking the whole building at its foundations.

Rhonda let out a strangled yell of surprise as Val threw the Cat into reverse, dragging her away from the wreck.

Val leaned out the cab, and yelled, "You okay?!"

"Not even close!" she wheezed back but managed a shaky thumbs-up.

He slammed the throttle again.

"Let's go!"

Below, the creatures were still attacking. Tentacles burst from the mud, coiling up around the treads, slithering through the bulldozer's gears. One slammed against the cab window, leaving a smear of foul slime behind. But they were just flesh against thick reinforced steel.

Val didn't wait around.

The vehicle surged forward with the groan of metal meeting resistance, then victory. The creatures, realizing what they were up against, gave way rather than be crushed. Their limbs recoiled, snapping back into the earth.

Up on the storage shed roof, Melvin was dancing like a lunatic, waving his arms and hopping in place. He pointed at the ground and laughed. "You can't stop us, you dumb Goddamn worms!"

He waved to the Cat. "Way to go Val," he shouted. "Now haul ass over here, man! Me next! Get me outta here!"

Val heard him and nodded. He steered the machine around to the storage shed, as the long trailer clanked behind him.

"Hell yeah!" Melvin couldn't help but cry out, realizing that he was about to be saved.

Just as the bulldozer eased alongside the shed, as Melvin grinned ecstatically, the small shed started to move, creak, then shudder.

The Graboid now struck.

A thunderous noise erupted as the creature exploded up through the base of the shed. Its wooden walls crumpled outward like ripping paper, and the entire roof dropped down with a metallic smash. Melvin yelped, falling with it.

Immediately, Val jumped out from the cab onto the edge of the bulldozer, boots slamming down on the metal. He reached down a hand.

"Grab on!" he yelled.

Rhonda could only stare from the cab, helpless to do anything.

Melvin grasped desperately at Val in terror, but the ground beneath him undulated.

The Graboid jerked up violently, bucking the roof that lay on it like a saddle, pulling away desperately.

Before he was pulled away with the roof, Melvin had managed to grab Val's hand, and now the creature moved, he moved too, pulling Val with him.

He landed beside Melvin on the small metal roof, just as the creature pitched and rolled beneath them. The corrugated metal flexed over the beast and moved like a furious bronco, bouncing and twisting with rage, unable to shake them.

Val and Melvin clung to the edge of the roof for dear life, straddling it like it was a curved seesaw. Beneath them, the monster thrashed again, and again. But the roof was too light, too pliable. It bent but didn't break, and the creature could not get out from underneath it.

Dirt sprayed up around them as Val grabbed onto the now screaming Melvin. The roof slid across the ground like a violent sled ride.

Then, just ahead, lay a drainage ditch.

As the creature approached, it moved deep down, and the sheet metal was thrown forward and plunged over the ditch's edge. Val and Melvin were thrown off from it, crashing in a heap at the muddy bottom.

Val quickly got to his feet.

"We've got about two seconds!" he shouted.

Spotting an irrigation pipe overhead he grabbed Melvin and shoved him upward. The boy jumped and grabbed for it, feet swinging.

Val leapt after him, just in time.

The Graboid then burst from the wall behind them, a roaring, blind fury of tentacles and muscle, but missed completely. It blasted out one side of the dirt ditch and collided into the far side with a crunch, vanishing beneath the dirt. Burrowing fast.

From the ditch's edge above them, the bulldozer's scoop appeared.

Earl was driving now.

"Well, come on, stop makin' out you two!" he shouted.

At Nancy's house, she and Mindy stood in relief watching the bulldozer approach. Allowing themselves to stop gripping each other so tightly. For the first time in hours, they could breathe without tears.

On the top of Burt and Heather's compound, the sound of the bulldozer drifting from the town was both unexpected and confusing. The couple paused what they were doing.

They were busily sawing heavy PVC pipes into short sections, filling them carefully with homemade explosives: mixtures of household chemicals, fertilizer, black powder, and a wealth of old-school know-how. Each pipe was packed with buckshot consisting of old nails, bolts and ball bearings, then sealed tight with their caps glued on. All put together with extreme care and caution.

Burt could not help but laugh as the bulldozer appeared over the horizon, dragging the trailer behind it.

"Well, I'll be damned," he said, impressed. "We got ourselves an armored transport."

The bulldozer rolled past the Gummer's now half-buried Blazer. Its chains rattling, trailer squealing in the dirt, as dust swirled in its wake.

Earl was still driving.

Val climbed up onto the roll cage above the cab, so he was nearly eye-level with Burt and Heather.

Below, the ground shook, as one of the creatures ineffectually slammed into the Cat. Val held on, riding out the impact. Knowing now that their attempts did little to stop them.

"Let's go you two!" he said over the noise of the bashing. "We're headed for the mountains!"

Burt didn't budge. He and Heather were still working, gluing another cap onto a fresh pipe bomb. "In a minute." He said, holding one of his PVC bombs, with his Dremel tool in his other hand, as he drilled a hole into the cap.

"Come on, Burt," Val said. "We can't hold on long. They're damn smart and getting smarter by the minute. Just 'cause they haven't beaten the Cat yet means squat. We gotta hurry!"

Burt grabbed a coil of fuse, cut off a length and fed it onto the bomb. "That's fine, we got some new things to teach 'em too."

Rhonda, behind the driver's seat, looked up to Val. "They're digging under us right now!"

Sure enough, the bulldozer tilted sideways, just slightly, but enough to feel.

"See that?" Earl shouted. "They're doing it! They're trying to sink us every time we hold still. Now let's *go!*"

Burt and Heather looked down off the roof and saw the Cat dipping in the sand.

Earl punched the throttle, and the rig drove out of the depression the creatures had carved.

Burt and Heather handed the crate of the finished bombs down to Val who handed them down to Rhonda, who handed them down to Miguel who was on top of the trailer with Nancy, Mindy and Melvin.

The Gummers then began grabbing everything they had amassed on their roof: weapons, ammo, snacks, gear, and even a cooler of beer. Val stood below like a bellhop, catching every armload, then passing them all down.

"Jesus Christ," Val muttered. "We're only going nine miles."

Burt didn't stop. "Yeah, well, those things are gonna be on our ass every foot of the way, right?"

He held up two rifles to Heather, an HK91 assault rifle and a monster of an elephant gun.

"What do you think? Max firepower or…?"

Heather barely hesitated. "Penetration all the way. The 458 shooting solids, less ammo to carry anyway."

Burt nodded.

Val shook his head, clutching the last sack of provisions like groceries. "Come on!"

Voices rose from the trailer and cab.

"Who cares?!"

"Forget that stuff!"

"Let's *go* already!"

Another slam shook the ground. Another plume of dust billowed up. Those on the trailer huddled closer.

Finally, Heather and Burt leapt down onto the scoop and climbed down onto the trailer, dragging the last of their supplies with them.

As he saw them both and their amount of weaponry, Melvin smiled. "Give me a gun, Burt! I'll take one!"

Burt barely looked at the boy. "I wouldn't give you a gun if it was World War Three."

With that, Earl floored the throttle, and the rig tore forward, flattening Burt's chain link fence as it went.

The Gummers looked back, watching their home recede into the dust. The fortress they'd spent years building, that they swore they would never abandon.

"Food for five years," Burt mumbled quietly to his wife. "A thousand gallons of gas. Air filtration. Water filtration. Geiger counter. Bomb shelter…"

He looked up at the sky.

"…and we get underground Goddamn monsters."

Heather slipped her arm around him and gave him a tight squeeze.

They rolled on along as the day, though starting to fade, was still a furnace.

The road trailed ahead in a rough, uneven line through the cliffs. Rocks jutted out across every part of this stretch, making the bulldozer's path more precarious as it dragged the trainer over the bumpy terrain. It lumbered forward, slow yet determined. This made for a strange convoy, but it was still working.

Inside the cab, Earl kept his hands tight on the levers, gritting his teeth as he hit rock after rock and the vehicle lurched along with it.

Val sat next to him, rifle laid across his lap. A cigarette was tucked behind his ear, one he'd long since forgotten to light. He was nervous but didn't want to show it to anyone.

Rhonda sat wedged between them, keeping her eyes on the horizon.

Outside, Burt rode in the bulldozer's scoop, keeping his eye on the land ahead with his gun held at the ready.

Heather sat astride the rear of the trailer, looking back, the elephant gun in her grip.

It was afternoon now, and the golden light cast the desert into a canvas of shadow and flame colors. The cliffs that rose up either side of them got darker as the sun started to lower.

For the first time in what felt like hours, there was a lull. A moment where each one of them believed that they could win this. Aside from Earl, who expected a Graboid to jump out from behind every rock, or burst up through every patch of clear ground.

He leaned back and called to the trailer behind them. "Any sign of 'em?"

Miguel's voice came back, tinged with a forced optimism. "Maybe they just gave up, you know? Maybe the dozer's too much for them. We know they ain't stupid."

Melvin, smirked. "Yeah, man. Maybe they can't handle our shit. We bring da bomb!"

In front, Burt in the scoop, pointed excitedly ahead.

"There we go," he called, voice raised over the growl of the engine. "Solid rock ahoy!"

Cheers rose from the trailer. Even Earl let himself grin.

But then Heather raised her arm. "No, wait… What's *that*?" she pointed off to the right.

From behind a large tumble of boulders, a thick plume of dust was rising, twisting upward in a column.

Everyone stared uneasily at the cloud.

Nancy whispered, "Is it them? It is, isn't it?"

Heather didn't take her eyes off it. "Well, what else could it be?"

From beside her, Mindy peered out from behind her mother. "What are they doing?"

"Maybe they're eating each other?" Melvin pondered, hopeful and half-joking.

In the cab, Rhonda turned to Val. "We don't have to go that way, right?"

"No." Val shook his head. "We stay straight."

"Damnit," Earl said through his teeth. "What the hell *are* they doing? They're up to something."

"I don't care what they're doing," Val said, "as long as they keep doing it way over there."

Earl shoved the throttle all the way, and the

bulldozer roared louder, treads digging into the earth as they moved on. The mountain wasn't far now.

Below the rising cloud plume, dirt was flying by the ton out of a hole in the ground, five feet wide, and very deep. A giant mound of dirt was piled high all around it, and down in the hole two large creatures dug, determined.

They should have turned around, but no one had expected the ground to give way beneath them. The bulldozer got less than fifty feet further before the dirt caved inward and the front end of the machine dropped heavily into a small pit, slamming with a jarring force. The Cat tipped forward as the trailer behind jackknifed, swinging before crashing to a stop on the very edge of this new sinkhole. Everyone was still on top of it, hanging on.

Inside the cab, everything was launched forward. Earl's head slammed against the levers. Rhonda flew hard into the dashboard, and Earl was flung against her, the wind knocked out of him.

The dozer's engine gave a desperate cough, then died.

Then came the voices. Shouting and scared.

"Burt!" Val yelled, climbing out the broken cab window to the scoop.

There was no sign of him.

"Burt!" Heather cried out, her hands and face scraped and sore from the collision.

Then, from the side of the cab, a hand reached up for assistance. Burt, with a face scratched and dusty, yet unhurt, looked up at Val.

"A little help?" he asked.

Val grabbed his arm and pulled him in. Burt nodded in thanks.

They all climbed back onto the trailer, where the others were gathered, bruised and shaken.

"They… Dug a damn trap!" Earl said in astonishment, shaking the daze from his mind.

"I can't believe this!" Val added.

"Typical VC-style move," Burt said with some disgust in his voice as he hugged his wife. "Dig a trench under a road and wait for us to drive right over. Should have predicted that. Coward's move."

Just as he spoke, the trailer sank to one side.

Below them, the ground wasn't stable. It was moving.

Dust boiled up around the base as the creatures now returned to finish their work. They were down, digging, and fast.

The trailer then shuddered, as the trailer began to sink.

Val and Earl grabbed the nearest of Burt and Heather's rifles. They then began firing into the ground around the trailer, but this was pointless. The bullets hardly penetrated the sand. The sound of them echoed uselessly around the narrow cliff walls.

Burt appeared between them, pulling out one of the makeshift pipe bombs from his overloaded knapsack. He quickly lit the fuse. "Hungry?" he growled as he turned to the nearest patch of churning earth. He hurled the bomb as hard as he could at it. "Eat this you commie bastards!" He then ducked. "Get down," he commanded everyone, just as the ground erupted.

Kaboom!

The explosion tore a crater into the dirt, sending chunks of earth and of dust into the air. A terrible noise followed. It didn't sound like anger. It sounded like pain. An animalistic cry of agony.

The trailer immediately stopped shaking.

After a few moments, everyone looked up over the edge. Hopeful that this may have done it.

"There they are!" Rhonda said, motioning behind them.

In the distance, two narrow trails of dust sped away down the trail.

"Hey Burt," Miguel said. "Did you get one of 'em?"

"No, there's still two," Rhonda said motioning to their retreat. "See? There's like two different dust trails there."

"Sure as hell got their attention, though," Val said. "What's in those things, Burt?"

"Just a few household chemicals in the proper proportion" he replied, as if that explained everything.

Heather turned to Earl. "What about the bulldozer? It's totaled?"

As everyone was watching the fleeing Graboids, Earl

had already surveyed the damage. The front end had vanished beneath the surface, the scoop buried, and the engine was still. "Ain't no way we're going anywhere in this," he said. "It's down for the count."

Val looked to the west, beyond the cliffs next to them. A rough line of boulders and jagged stone stood proudly.

"If we make it there," he said. "We're safe."

But Rhonda was already looking back at the dust.

"Oh shit, here they come… They're coming back."

Heather stepped up, raised the elephant gun at the oncoming dust, and fired two deafening shots at them, more out of frustration than expecting to hit them. The recoil rocked her backward, and the creatures didn't slow.

"Save the ammo," Burt said, grabbing her arm.

Val shouted "Come on, everybody! To the rocks!"

"Jesus, Val," Earl said. "That's a long way."

"We'll never make it," Melvin shouted. "They'll get us for sure!"

"They'll sure as hell get us if we stay here," Val said. "Better we at least try."

"Wait, wait," Rhonda said, turning to Burt. "Do you have another one of those bombs?"

Burt was already holding one in his hands. "I have one or two, or three, or four," he smiled.

She pointed at the rocks to where they were going. "Well, what if you threw one that way. The way we want to go. Then, when it explodes, it could drive them away, thinking they're in danger again, and we run like goddamn bastards!" She turned to Earl. "Pardon my French."

Val couldn't hold in his laugh. Earl didn't appreciate the mockery. It was short lived though as the trailer juddered, as the Graboids returned to their work, sinking them deeper into the dirt.

"What if it doesn't scare them away?" Melvin said. "What if they don't run?"

"I don't think it does scare them," she said. "The sound *hurts* them. It's not fear. It's pain. They're so sensitive to sound, they can hear the slightest vibration. The sound of these things must be too much."

Everyone turned to each other, wondering if it could be true.

Burt nodded. "Well, she's got my vote."

"Right. We're gonna run, get ready," Val said as he noticed Mindy, trembling behind Nancy, tears pouring through the dust on her cheeks. He squatted down beside her, smiling as if the trailer wasn't sinking further or that the two monsters were not attacking.

"You understand what we're gonna do?" he asked softly.

She nodded.

"We get to the rocks. We're safe. That's all you have to think about."

Melvin's voice came again, trembling. "I don't know man.... They're too fast... You can't outrun them, no way... We—"

Burt pressed a massive revolver into Melvin's hand

to shut him up. A Ruger Super Redhawk .44 Magnum. A beast of a gun.

"Here," he smiled. "This'll make 'em think twice."

Melvin stared at the weapon, bug-eyed with excitement, before happily taking it.

Burt then lit the fuse on his next bomb. "Heads down for a full house," he shouted, hurling the bomb in a long arc toward the rocks ahead of them.

A beat.

Another beat.

Kaboom!

The rocks around it started to fall, as another unearthly shriek of pain sounded from below the ground. A shriek that then backed away down the trail.

Rhonda stood as she saw the dust trails rising off the dirt again, both Graboids scurrying away in retreat. "It worked. There they go!"

Val didn't hesitate.

"*Let's do it*!"

And like that, they ran.

All of them.

Burt cried out as they surged off the half-sunk trailer like trench soldiers. Weapons clutched, they charged forward into this no man's land, up the dirt trail. Melvin ran like his life depended on it, because it did. He raised the revolver back toward the retreating monsters, and in an act of defiance, pulled the trigger.

Click.

He tried again. *Click. Click.*

"Burt, you bastard!" he shouted, and ran even faster, trying to overtake them all.

Behind, Nancy struggled with Mindy. The girl was flagging, stumbling. Nancy tried to pull her along.

Val and Earl swooped in without missing a step, lifting Mindy between them, one under each arm.

Ahead, the rocks waited.

Behind them, the ground screamed, as the monsters were in a fury, turning back.

CHAPTER 9

A BRILLIANTLY STUPID IDEA

Huge slabs of outcrop stuck out, slanting upward into the sky. It was a sanctuary of solid ground surrounded by an ocean of treacherous sand. They all reached it in a scramble, clambering up onto the stone with mutual cries of relief.

Melvin, panting, his face red, stormed straight at Burt, pushing the .44 Magnum back into his hands.

"You asshole!" he screamed. "There's no bullets in this thing!"

Burt didn't even flinch. "Well, got you moving, didn't it?"

A few people laughed, but it was quickly forgotten, as tentacles surged up on two sides of the rock. They burst up out of the sand and swept blindly across the edges of the outcrop. Pulsing and flexing as they reached and probed.

Burt already had one of his bombs in hand, ready to

throw it again. But as their screams died out, the group soon realized that while the threat was terrifying, the creatures could not reach them. They were in no immediate danger.

"So... now what?" Earl asked, his voice intentionally quiet. As if the Graboids could listen and understand.

Rhonda turned to the distant mountains. "Could we make it there?" she asked.

"No way," Val said. He gestured at Burt's few remaining bombs. "We'd need another fifty of those things. The Cat was supposed to get us at least another mile. We're lucky as shit this was here."

Earl let out a loud sigh and crouched down. "Well... that's it. We're not getting off this rock..."

Val glanced around at the miles of surrounding desert. "Can't pole vault anywhere, either. That's for sure."

"What's the matter with you?" Heather spoke up, clearly annoyed." What are you even talking about? You don't give up in a war. You fight. You fight 'til they fall down. They die just like we all do."

"They're prehistoric," Rhonda replied. "They'll just wait out there 'til we starve to death."

The silence deepened as the reality and futility of their situation sank in.

Burt lost his cool, his voice loud. "What? Well, for Christ's sake, we could have made a stand at our place! We had food, heat, water..."

"You can't fight 'em that way," Earl snapped back.

But Burt wasn't listening. "You two jerkoffs hauled us way the hell out here!"

Val stepped between them, his own anger bubbling. "Back off, Burt! We could've just left you two stuck on your roof!"

"I wish you had! Who the hell put you two in charge?!"

"Burt!" Nancy cut in, louder. She was a woman who rarely raised her voice, but when she did, it commanded attention. "Those things would have *killed* you, don't you get it? You are not invincible."

Burt was surprised into silence. Nancy's voice softened, but it still carried.

"You haven't seen what they can do. They would have flattened your home with you in it."

Earl looked at her and nodded slowly. "They'd have dug your place out from under you in less than half an hour. We've seen 'em do it."

No one spoke.

The wind scuttled across the rock, as the last hours of heat beat down upon them. They each soon slumped where they had stood, some alone, some huddled close.

Burt knelt, turning one of his bombs over in his hand, his fingers restless. He was agitated, annoyed, and just plain pissed off. Not just at anyone in particular, not at the monsters, but all of it. At the fact he was here and was not already victorious. After a while, he looked up and spoke quietly.

"If it comes to starvation, I know what *I'm* doing." He motioned to the bomb in his hand. "I'm gonna take one of these. Walk *right out* there with the fuse lit. Stuff it down my pants and let 'em take me down...." He grinned grimly. "*BOOOOM* they all fall dead."

Heather moved to his side and put her hand on his back. "Jesus, honey, no," she said in a whisper.

But Earl, who had been quiet for a while, looked up. Something in his expression changed. "You know, that's not a half-bad idea."

The others turned to him, with shocked expressions. Even Burt.

"No, I mean it gives me an idea... going fishing like..."

Burt looked at his bomb, then at Earl. His bleak expression turned into an excitable smile as he knew exactly what the plan was.

In the open desert to one side of the outcrop, a rock landed in the sand with a thud.

Then another.

Val and Rhonda stood at the edge, hurling rock after rock into the open desert, each one arcing high before smacking down into the sand. Every thud sent up a small cloud around it.

In front of them, on a lower ledge, Earl crouched with Burt. He had a coil of nylon rope from one of the packs, and Burt was securing one of his bombs to its end. The rest of them were tucked safely away behind a pile of rock ten feet away, as far from harm as they could manage.

Meanwhile Val and Rhonda kept the rocks flying through the air, thumping onto the sand.

Soon, the ground moved in front of them.

Val let fly another rock. It struck and rolled, and the ground near it rippled.

"There," he said, pointing. "Right straight out in front of you, twenty feet."

Burt measured the spot with his eyes, then leaned closer to Earl. "How much do you think?"

"I don't know," Earl said. "They're pretty quick… maybe fifteen seconds?"

Burt nodded. He measured out a length of fuse and clipped it clean. Knowing exactly how much was needed. As he worked it into the bomb, Earl watched him.

"What the hell is that stuff, anyway?" he asked.

"Cannon fuse," Burt said, not looking up.

"What do *you* use that for?"

Burt stopped and turned, looking confused, as if that was a strange question. But his answer was even more strange. "I use it for my cannon."

The bomb was ready. Earl patted down his pockets for a lighter, but Val already had it in hand. He stepped up, leaning down to light the fuse, but frowned as he saw how Earl was holding the rope.

"Come on, you're not gonna do your rope thing, are you?"

Earl smiled cockily. "Hey, just 'cause you're no good at it."

Shaking his head, Val lit the fuse.

Fifteen.

Immediately Earl stood and began to spin the rope overhead, the bomb whirling in a wide circle above, just like it was a lasso.

Eleven.

Ten.

As it built up speed, he soon let it fly, as far as he could throw. It soared high, trailing fuse smoke behind it, and landed with a puff in the sand.

Eight.

Seven.

He paused for a second before he started reeling it back in, dragging it across the dust in short, jerky motions like a lure. The fuse, loud and fizzing.

Five.

They crouched down behind the largest slab of rock and waited.

Rhonda checked her watch. "Come on... come on..."

Four.

Earl peeked out from behind the rock and pulled the bomb in a bit closer.

Burt's eyes were locked on the ground. "Take it... take the bait..."

Three.

A mound began to rise underneath the bomb, as one of the creature's snouts surfaced. The boney mandibles opened, swallowing in one quick gulp.

Two.

One.

Kaboom!

The explosion tore up the desert floor. Sand, smoke, and chunks of the creature sprayed skyward in a grotesque geyser. Masses of orange blooded meat hit the rocks with sickening splats. The monster had exploded.

From behind, across the outcrop where people hid, came wild cheering.

Everyone had seen it.

The next bomb was already being tied. Earl worked quickly, looping the rope with anxious hands while Val and Rhonda searched for the target. Another rock was hurled, then another. They waited for movement.

Nothing.

Then another was thrown.

Nothing.

"Where the hell is he?" Earl said. "Hope he didn't wise up."

A moment later, Rhonda threw a rock and smiled as it landed. "Nope. Right there," she pointed.

From the earth came a half tentacle. Severed from a previous encounter. Axle.

Val grinned and reached for the bomb. "Well, well. well, look who it is… This prick is mine."

He took the explosive from Earl and handed the lighter to Rhonda. Holding the explosive ready to throw, she shakily lit it with a mix of nerves and anxiety.

The fuse lit.

Everyone dropped into their hiding places behind various rocks and ledges.

Fourteen.

Thirteen.

Val hurled it with the same motion, same timing, same arc as Earl had done, holding onto the other end of the rope. It landed with a thump on a clean piece of sand, and he began to pull it, crawling back across the ground.

Nine.

All eyes were fixed on the bomb. The fuse sparked and smoked.

Eight.

The ground underneath it surged up.

Seven.

The bomb sank inward. Swallowed deep.

Six.

"Yes!" Burt cried out.

Five.

"We got it," Earl said.

Four.

From out of the ground, the bomb came back. Hurtling upwards into the air, spat back at them with force.

It flew high, straight at the outcrop, the fuse still lit.

Two.

Before they had a chance to find cover, the bomb soared over their heads in a spinning blur and struck the rock wall behind them. It bounced once, then skittered down a narrow crack. Between the slabs, it disappeared from view…

…straight into the pile of unused bombs. The same bombs that had been hidden there for safety.

Val, Rhonda and Earl scattered, as Burt dove backward over the rock's edge.

Heather, Nancy, Mindy, Miguel and Melvin ran higher up the outcrop.

Everything stopped for that last second.

Everyone held their breath.

BABABAMMM!

The blast shattered the outcrop, as stone and fire blasted skyward. The air itself shook as a shockwave emanated from the large collection of munitions.

In the desert, the creature streaked away in fear of the immense noise.

When the sound cleared and the dust settled, Val groaned and rolled over, coughing.

He and Earl were not on solid ground. They were far out in the open desert.

So was Rhonda, sprawled across a flat patch of sand, close by.

Out of the four of them, only Burt had stayed on the outcrop, safely on the lower ledge he had dropped to.

Everyone else was unharmed and looked helplessly from the top of the rock.

Val, Earl and Rhonda looked at each other, then

immediately around them. They could feel a deep hum rumbling beneath the sand. Getting stronger. But could not see where the creature was.

"Run!" Val shouted, as the three got to their feet and started sprinting back to the broken outcrop.

"Breach!" Burt shouted as he ran back up the rock, pointing to the sand between them.

The ground in front of the rock broke apart as the Graboid, Axle, burst out, roaring. Their path back to safety was cut off.

Immediately they all stopped in their tracks.

On the rocks, looking down, Heather took aim. Her voice rang out across the desert. "Make noise," She screamed to the others behind her. "Everybody! *Come on!*"

Her gunshots cracked in the air, as Miguel, Melvin, Mindy and Nancy all stomped their feet, shouted, whistled. They threw rocks out into the sand ahead in a flurry.

But the lurching creature did not pay them any attention. It just hovered for a second, looking at Val, Rhonda and Earl, before slowly sinking back into its hole.

Burt ran to the edge, the elephant rifle in hand, aimed at the dirt.

"Come on, you slimebag," he seethed. "Over here… Fresh meat! I got a nice present for ya!"

Earl made a move to the rocks, but Val grabbed his arm.

"Wait. He's expecting that. He's the smart one. He's trying to trick us."

Earl replied in a nervous whisper. "Well, we use this then!" he said, lifting a pipe bomb. "Good thing I still have this."

"It's our last one," Val said, unsure.

"What else you gonna do with it? Marry it?"

Val took a breath. "Look, so we get back on that rock and in three days we're dead anyway."

"I *want* to live for those three days, if it's alright by you. Don't wanna end it today!"

From the rocks, Burt shouted over. "What's wrong? Use the bomb, for *God's sake*!"

Val stared at the dirt, forcing himself to believe his words "He *can't* be smarter than us. He just can't."

"Come on, let's do it!" Earl insisted.

Val suddenly raised his hand up for silence. Which everyone did. Including those on the rocks.

"Don't move," Val whispered. "I'm gonna go for it."

Earl looked at him. "Go for *what*?!"

But Val was already moving, and he snatched the bomb out of Earl's hand. He had turned and run… *away* from the outcrop.

The ground exploded behind them, as the creature lunged in a cloud of sand and hunger.

"Shit!" Earl screamed, as he jumped back in shock, having no other option than to follow his friend. Rhonda, further away, had no idea what to do, as the creature passed unaware she was there.

"What the hell are you doing?!" Earl screamed out to Val as they ran.

"I got a plan!" he shouted back, sounding giddy with excitement.

As Earl caught up, they ran together, sand flying from their heels, out of breath. Val reached into his pockets, frantically searching. No lighter.

Earl checked his own.

Their faces fell.

The roar of the creature in pursuit sounded behind them.

Rhonda quickly realized that she had the lighter.

"I've got it! I've got it!" she shouted, grabbing it from her pocket and holding it aloft, before breaking into a sprint.

She was a faster runner than either Val or Earl and didn't rely on a beer and cigarette diet. She raced in a wide circle around the creature's path and caught up to them. She held the lighter out to the fuse.

"Not yet," Val said, pulling the bomb away.

Ahead, a massive cliff loomed. A sheer drop down into a deep canyon below. A clear thousand-foot drop. No way around. This was the end of the line.

"This better be one great plan, Val!" Earl shouted.

They skidded to the edge, and Val took the fuse between his teeth and bit most of it off, leaving only an inch. He looked up, expecting the creature to be on their heels, but it was not. Not anymore. It had slowed down, still advancing through the dirt, but taking its time.

"It could have caught up easily," Earl said. "Why didn't it?"

Val smirked. "Bastard thinks its toying with us. Playing with its food."

"It's probably cautious," Rhonda said, hoping she was the right one. "After all, we killed the others."

"Get ready!" Val said as he held out the bomb to her.

Quickly Rhonda went to light it, but Val grabbed her wrist.

"Not yet… *not yet…*" he said.

"Light it, man! *Light it*!" Earl urged.

The Graboid started to get faster. Breaking through the surface the nearer it got. Val's jaw clenched.

He let go of her wrist. "Now!" he shouted.

She lit the flame. The fuse caught light and sparked.

He then hurled the bomb high…

…right past the creature.

Behind it as it came faster and faster toward them.

Earl looked aghast. "Too far! You missed it!"

They broke off and ran in different directions, left and right away from the cliff's edge.

Val, though, didn't move.

Kaboom!

The explosion shook the canyon floor.

The Graboid screamed in terror.

It bolted forward, straight at Val, away from the blast, away from the pain…

… straight to the cliff's edge.

The earth heaved; a wall of sand raced at Val like a tidal wave.

Val stood his ground, as the creature rose up, mouth wide. Aiming for Val, in pain from the sound. Totally confused and in a rage.

Val jumped clear at the very last second. Letting the hump of dirt and monster zoom straight past him.

The edge of the cliff came up fast, a sheer drop into open air.

The creature didn't stop. Couldn't stop. The sound of the bomb still searing through its sensitive nerves.

It burst from the earth, roaring through the edge in a thunderous spray of rock and sand. For a frozen instant it hung in the air, suspended like the monstrous, twisted leviathan it was, its body still rippling and writhing from the blast.

Then gravity took a firm and unforgiving hold.

It fell.

Fast.

The scream it let out echoed over the desert as its long, segmented form fell downward, flailing against the open air as it plunged down and down. And there, at the bottom, it met ferociously with the rocks.

The impact was terrible.

The creature exploded against the jagged stones, its body bursting in a wet, meaty eruption of gore. Bits of it scattered across the ravine walls in a blast of multi-colored flesh and orange blood. Its final shriek echoed throughout the canyon even after its body had been decimated on impact.

· · ·

From above, three figures stood at the brink, looking down.

Val didn't move, he just stared at the mess far below. He stood there for a long moment. He didn't speak. He just watched, his hands on his knees, lungs heaving as they caught his breath.

Rhonda and Earl had turned to look at him with disbelief and amazement, not just at what had happened, but at him.

Val finally looked up and saw them staring. There was a pause, and then, almost sheepishly, he said, "Well, it just suddenly hit me, you know? Stampede?"

They stared a beat longer, then started to laugh.

It began as a chuckle and rolled into something uncontrollable. The kind of laughter that only comes when fear finally breaks. The three turned and started the long walk back to the others, their steps cautious at first. Then Val began exaggerating his footfall, stomping across the sand. Unafraid.

Rhonda and Earl followed, mimicking his steps. They walked arm in arm, stomping merrily across the desert.

Back in Perfection, the town was still a broken mess. Roofs caved in, fences flattened, porches half-sunk, but life was safe again, and the sun had finally started to set, after a long and frankly terrifying day.

They had all made their way back, and slept a deep, well-earned sleep. Even Burt and Heather decided to stay in town that night. Finding security with others they hadn't felt before. And when the morning came again, they all got up and didn't know quite what to do.

Most stayed in their houses, quiet, wondering what would come next.

Val and Earl were wide awake and already putting a plan into action. They walked confidently down the main street, rolling two scavenged tires toward their own truck, which stood on cinder blocks outside the collapsed remnants of Walter Chang's store.

Mindy shot past them in a blur.

"Look!" she shouted.

From around the bend, a battered highway maintenance truck crested the ridge, followed closely by a sheriff's cruiser. Both vehicles slowed as they approached, the people inside shocked at seeing the devastation and taking it all in.

The maintenance truck pulled to a stop. Two road workers climbed down slowly. Behind them, the sheriff's cruiser pulled in, and out stepped a tall man in mirrored sunglasses and a pristine uniform. He was mid-forties, with silver at his temples. A shorter, younger deputy climbed out after him, open mouthed at the state of the small town.

For a moment, nobody spoke.

Then, as the townsfolk came out of their houses and trailers to meet them, *everyone* spoke at once.

Miguel surged forward, arms waving in the air. "They came up out of the ground! Big sons of bitches! Ate Edgar, Walter and Old Fred and ripped out the foundations of our houses! They might even speak English, we don't know!"

Burt pushed past him, the splatter of blood still dried on his fatigues from the day before, a revolver tucked into his waistband. "I told you! Didn't I say we had to be prepared, Sheriff? This is why! *This* is why."

Heather stood beside him, trying to corral the more excitable voices. "Let them breathe, people, let them breathe!"

The sheriff took off his sunglasses slowly, gazing across the broken buildings, the cratered ground, and the now empty water tower. He was caught between disbelief and a headache.

"What the hell happened?" he said.

The deputy leaned closer to his superior. "Sir, is that… is that a snake?"

He was staring at the limp, dust-covered appendage sprawled across the road, half-coiled and reeking in the sun like a dead eel, the size of a firehose.

Earl walked over, with a confident smile.

"Well, Sheriff," he said, "you ain't gonna believe a word of it. But we had us a hell of a pest problem."

Behind, Val chuckled. "Underground slugs. Big ones. Meaner than hell. Tentacles and everything."

The sheriff stared silently. "And I suppose you're gonna tell me you all handled it."

Earl shrugged. "Sure did, it's how we're all here now."

The deputy nudged the sheriff, "Sir, we should probably call this in."

"You think?" the sheriff replied sarcastically, already feeling the stress of the paperwork ahead.

Rhonda, at the back of the crowd, raised her hand like she was in school. "We've got seismic records. I can explain what happened... scientifically. At least most of it."

The sheriff looked at her, and let out a long, slow sigh. "Alright," he said. "Somebody better start at the beginning."

Not wanting to get involved, Val tipped his hat. "You'll get the story. If you need us, we'll be in Bixby."

As he and Earl walked back to the truck, the townsfolk tried to explain at once, with waving arms, half-coherent yelling, and plenty of gestures at the dirt beneath them.

"Road's open I guess!" Earl said happily, as they began fitting the tires to the truck.

"Road's damn well open!" Val echoed. "Now, soon as we hit Bixby we start making phone calls. We could make some real money off this whole thing, get in People magazine..."

"People?" Earl grinned. "Hell, let's go for National Geographic."

"Sell the movie rights. We're going straight from blue-collar to white-collar. Get some big studio involved..."

"Yeah… sure… but we don't wear no ties."

"Hell no," Val laughed. "*No* ties."

As Rhonda's truck approached, their conversation fell silent. Val leaned in through his driver's side window, reached up to the sun visor, and yanked down the dog-eared bimbo photos that had been hanging there longer than he liked to admit. He crumpled them quietly and stuffed them behind the front seat before turning back around.

Earl caught the move and raised an eyebrow. He didn't say a word, but the toothy grin said plenty.

Rhonda rolled to a stop and leaned out her window, snapping their picture with a high-end camera.

"Burt loaned me this," she said, happily. "So, I can get pictures of the one we dug up."

Val looked at her, suddenly awkward. "Hi, Rhonda," he said.

"It's all pretty exciting, huh?" she said. "There's going to be major research up here. And I'm going to be in on it at ground level! I'm probably the only scientist to have seen one alive and survived!"

Val nodded, still tongue-tied. He opened his mouth, closed it again. There was a long pause, just long enough to become quite uncomfortable, for him anyway. She didn't realize.

"First thing is to get some pictures of that one, then at all the places it hit," she said. "And I gotta get all my readings for the Sheriff to look at."

"Pictures?" Val eventually replied, stumbling on the word. "That's good. Yeah, pictures are a good idea."

Earl stared, watching this unfold… or more like totally failing to. He stood dumbfounded as the most unkillable man in town went down in flames before his eyes.

Rhonda leaned out of her truck and offered her hand to him.

"Uh…well, maybe I'll see you around sometime…" she said. "And thanks for everything," she then whispered. "You know, saving my life and stuff."

Val shook her hand quickly. "Well… you're welcome and all that."

She gazed at him a moment longer. There was something there. But it passed. She snapped out of it.

"Well… see ya," she said, and looked over to Earl and smiled.

He nodded back.

Val just stood, watching her drive off.

Earl walked up beside him, arms crossed, chuckling. "You're kidding me," he said. "Really? *Really?*"

"What? Shut up, Earl." Val replied, annoyed.

Across the flat expanse of desert highway leading to Bixby, with its tires replaced, and a full tank of gas, the truck rumbled along.

Val and Earl drove in silence for a long time, the wind pouring in through the open windows, the new tires humming smoothly against the asphalt. A welcome feeling after the bumpy terrain they had driven over in Perfection.

Earl stared ahead, chewing on the words in his mouth. Wanting to tell Val how stupid he was. After a while, he just couldn't hold it in anymore.

"I just flat out don't believe it!" he blurted. "After five years, you finally take my advice; you fall for a quality woman. But then what do you do? You stand there doing nothing! Like a lump of cheese in the sun."

Val stared out of the window. "Earl, get real. Women like that do *not* go for guys like us."

Earl shot him a look. "Wait, first she wasn't good enough for you. Now *you're* not good enough for her?! Didn't we skip a step here?"

Val didn't answer.

"*You* don't decide if you're worthless," Earl said, exasperated. "*She* does."

"Look, if we're going to Bixby, let's just go to Bixby." Val was exasperated, not knowing what to do. "Too late to do anything now anyway. We're on our way."

Earl threw up his hands, defeated. He dug into his shirt pocket, pulled out a cigarette from the pack, and stuck it in his mouth. He reached into his other pocket, then the glovebox.

He then slowed the truck to a stop in the middle of the road.

"What is it?" Val asked, suddenly worried that there could be another Graboid somewhere that Earl had spotted.

"Son of a gun." A slow smile spread across Earl's face as he laughed. "You know that girl's still got our lighter, don't ya?"

"Oh yeah," Val replied, seeing where this was going.
"It's a damn good lighter too."

"Sure is… One of a kind."

The truck pulled into a wide U-turn across the road.

They turned back, once again headed for Perfection.

ECHO ON PUBLICATIONS

Official Novelizations
from Echo On Publication

In The Mouth
of Madness

Night of The Comet

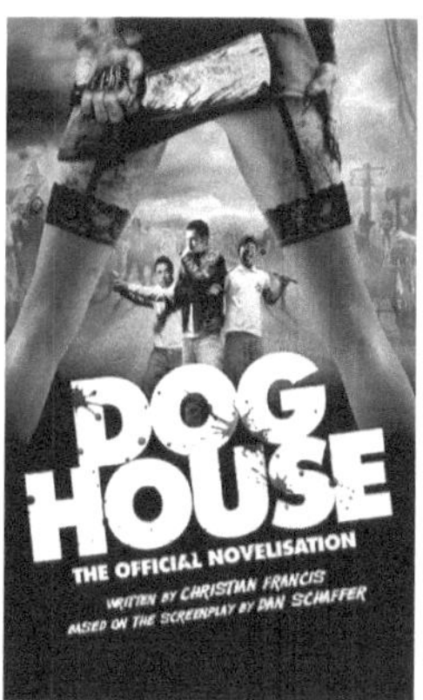

Doghouse

Witchboard

The Gate

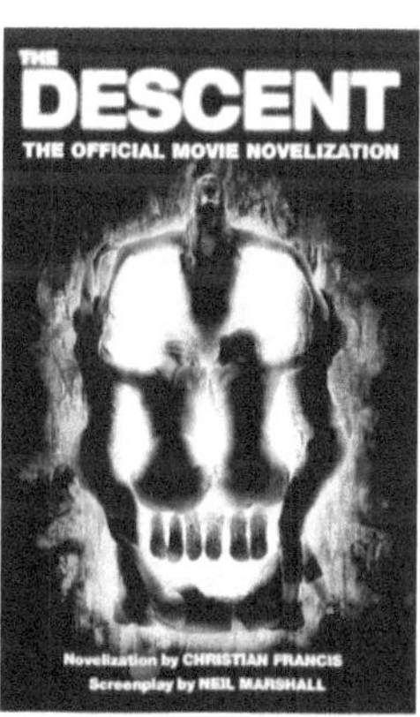

The Descent
*In Partnership with
Titan Books*

check echohorror.com for more details

Official Novelizations
from Echo On Publication

Beneath Perfectiion
(Tremors)

Session 9

The First Power

Maniac Cop 1,2 & 3
*Avaialble individually or as a
collected hardcover*

Dee Snider's
Strangeland

3615 Code
Santa Claus

check echohorror.com for more details

Original Novels and Novellas
by Christian Francis

The Dead Woods
YA Horror

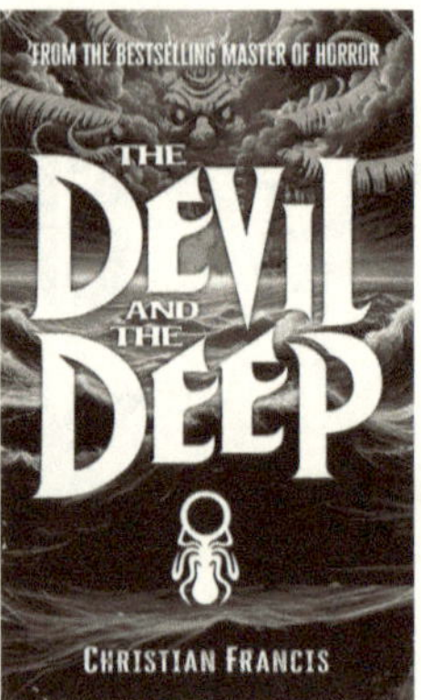

**The Devil
and The Deep**
Cosmic Horror

**The Sacrifice of
Anton Stacey**
Horror Novella

The Animus Chronicles Part 1
Everyday Monsters
Horror/Dark Fantasy

The Animus Chronicles Part 2
Incubus: The Descent
Horror/Dark Fantasy